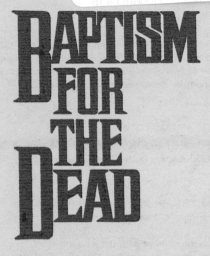

BAPTISM FOR THE DEAD

ROBERT IRVINE

POCKET BOOKS

New York   London   Toronto   Sydney   Tokyo   Singapore

POCKET BOOKS, a division of Simon & Schuster Inc.
1230 Avenue of the Americas, New York, NY 10020

Copyright © 1988 by R. R. Irvine
Cover art copyright © 1990 Ron Barbagallo

Published by arrangement with the author
Library of Congress Catalog Card Number: 88-16860

ISBN 0-671-69495-2

First Pocket Books printing February 1990

10 9 8 7 6 5 4 3 2 1

POCKET and colophon are registered trademarks of Simon & Schuster Inc.

Printed in the U.S.A

AN OUTCROPPING OF SANDSTONE EXPLODED NEAR HIS HEAD . . .

Shards of rock ripped open his cheek. An instant later the sound of the rifle shot arrived, a more deadly kind of thunder.

Traveler rolled to the back of the cave. Even there he was only a few feet from the edge of the butte. He felt helpless. The .45 in his hand was good only for close-in work.

Another shot dug sandstone from the red wall above him. Thunder shook the mountain. With it came rain, a sheet of water that sluiced down the mountainside, forming a curtain between Traveler and the sniper.

Traveler eased forward until he could cover the chimney approach, just in case the sniper might be foolish enough to try finishing the job in person. The movement started him sliding head-first on the wet sandstone. He caught himself just in time. With such treacherous footing no one would be coming after him. He wasn't going anywhere either . . .

To Annie K. Irvine,
my second mother
And to the memory of my father,
Garner D. "Jack" Irvine

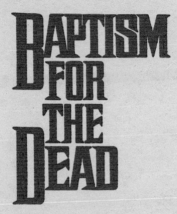

BAPTISM FOR THE DEAD

1

Storm clouds, the leading edge of what forecasters were calling the Yukon Express, abruptly snuffed out the sun, darkening Traveler's office. At the same moment the door opened. The woman who stood there, backlit from the hallway, wore a golden halo.

"Moroni Traveler?" she said as if she didn't believe the name on the door.

"That's right." He left his desk to switch on the overhead light, a pair of fluorescent tubes that blinked reluctantly before flaring to life.

Her halo became blond hair, real as far as he could tell.

"I called for an appointment," she said before closing the door behind her. "Penny Snow."

"I was expecting you, Miss Snow. Please have a seat."

She waited until he moved back behind his desk before sitting down. At first glance she looked very young, just out of high school perhaps, certainly no more than twenty. But her eyes belonged to someone older, blue and cold, with innocence long gone.

9

Thunder rumbled in the distance. She shivered. Her light spring suit, a two-piece tan seersucker with a frilly white blouse underneath, would be no match for the Yukon Express.

His deliberate stare caused her to fidget.

"I saw your ad in the phone book," she began quickly. "Your name caught my eye."

As a child growing up he'd caught hell because of that name.

She wrinkled her nose. "It smells funny in here."

"Gun oil. They're a hobby of mine." He indicated a small table near the window where pieces of a rifle lay on a drop cloth.

"I don't need that kind of help."

"On the phone," he prompted, "you said something about a missing person."

"My mother." She dug into a purse that didn't quite match her suit and slid a color snapshot across the dusty desktop. In it, a man and a woman stood side by side, though not quite touching each other. Both squinted at the camera, their faces distorted without revealing emotion.

"Your parents?"

"Yes. That was taken about six years ago, shortly before Mother went away."

Mother and daughter looked nothing alike. The older woman had dark hair, brown eyes, and no waist at all, just a straight line from shoulder to hips. It was a matter of genetics, not fat. The smile wrinkles around her mouth and eyes made him want to find her.

He smiled, impelling Penny to answer in kind. But her face didn't crease in the same places as her mother's.

"Tell me about her," he said.

"She left when I was fifteen. My father drove her away."

When she didn't continue immediately Traveler turned away to watch her reflection in the window directly behind his desk. The sky beyond the glass, filled with writhing thunderheads, threatened the stability of her image.

"My father is an official of *the* church," she said.

In Utah that meant the Church of Jesus Christ of Latter-day Saints. LDS for short, but more popularly known as Mormons.

"He's a member of the Council of Seventy," she added, a revelation that straightened his spine. A council member was only one step removed from the apostles who advised God's living prophet on earth.

"And he drove your mother away?" Traveler nudged gently.

"He and his holier-than-thou attitude."

"Does your father know you're here?"

"Does that make a difference?"

Traveler abandoned his chair to stand directly in front of the window.

"Look out there." He indicated the other window.

His was a corner office, northeast side, on the top floor of the Chester Building, directly across the street from the temple.

"What do you see?" he said.

"I don't know what you want me to say."

"Brigham Young's city. Salt Lake. His dream. His creation."

"I know the history. I was born here."

Traveler glanced from one window to the other.

Beyond the glass he could hear the wind picking up. To the east, still cloud-free and sunlit, stood the Wasatch Mountains, a ten-thousand-foot wall of gray granite peaks that looked as deadly as the jaws of some ancient carnivore.

Brigham Young had crossed those heights in 1847 to reach this, his promised land. He'd sought a place no one else wanted, a valley that would provide natural protection for his new religion.

"In case it's escaped your attention," he said, "we're living in a theocracy."

"Are you saying that you're afraid of my father and won't help me?"

He returned to his chair. Penny remained standing, her back to the window.

"I can't help anyone without more information."

"Of course. I'm being foolish." She sat down again, crossed one nyloned leg and then the other. Her mouth opened. She wet her lips. Instead of speaking she reached into her purse and came out with a box of menthol cigarettes. She lit one and then looked around for an ashtray. Seeing none she said, "I'm sorry. I didn't realize you were LDS."

"I'm not." He didn't equate smoking with hellfire the way Mormons did. On the other hand he didn't like breathing cancer by proxy either. But he kept the thought to himself, dumping pencils from a marmalade jar before handing it over as an ashtray.

She tapped her cigarette nervously against the jar and said, "My mother's name is Martha Varney."

The name Varney rang a bell. There'd been a Varney with Joseph Smith from the beginning, from Palmyra,

New York, when he founded the faith, to Missouri, and onto Nauvoo, Illinois, near where the first prophet of Mormonism was murdered. Since then Varneys had held any number of sacred points, including the rank of apostle.

"Her maiden name was Snow," Penny continued. "When she left, I wanted to go with her. But she wouldn't let me. I think she knew my father would never allow such a thing. He wouldn't even divorce her, you know. 'A man who speaks for the church,' he told me, 'cannot be tarnished.' Do you believe that, in this day and age?"

She stopped talking to draw smoke into her lungs. Only a trace came out when she continued. "Divorce wouldn't prevent a man from remarrying in the temple. But the rules are different for women. One temple marriage is the limit for us second-class citizens."

She lit a new cigarette from the old. "I did this in front of my father once. I thought he was going to have a heart attack right there on the spot."

"You're getting off the track."

She blew smoke at him and shook her head. "My father is the point. None of this would have happened without him."

"When did you start calling yourself Snow?"

"When I left home."

Traveler reached back to open the window behind him. The sudden rush of air was unexpectedly cold but at least made breathing easier.

"How long since you've seen your mother?"

"I didn't see her after she left. 'Once you walk out of this house,' he told her, 'I don't want you crawling back.' I don't know if my mother was afraid of him then, but I was. She promised to write to me every week, though. She did, too, until about six months ago."

"What happened then?"

"You have to understand. My father always opens my letters. For all I know she's still writing but he won't let me see them."

"Have you asked him about it?"

A smoky sigh escaped her. "He says no. That's what's got me so worried. My father is a lot of things, but not a liar."

"Where did your mother's letters come from?"

"The last few years the postmarks were Lydel Springs, Arizona."

"Have you checked there?"

"I called the sheriff. He was nice enough but couldn't tell me anything. You see, Mother joined one of those fundamentalist groups that think the church has strayed from its true path. I think she did it to spite my father."

Penny's fingers trembled as she lit another menthol. "It's all a sham, you know. The church. Everything. If there was a God, He wouldn't put up with all this crap." She waved toward the window, a defiant gesture condemning Brigham Young's legacy. But tears were running down her cheeks.

"Something must have happened to my mother. Otherwise she would never have stopped writing." Penny stabbed out her cigarette. "I dream about her every night. It's always the same. She's burning in hell because she never joined the church, another reason my father refused to get a divorce. People always said his marrying outside the faith would be his undoing. So he's not about to give them the satisfaction of divorce. Whenever anybody asks him about my mother, he looks contrite and says, 'I'm praying for her to come back to God.' "

She clenched her fists until they shook. "There was a time when I begged him to have her baptized in absentia. You know about that, don't you?"

He nodded. Mormons were obsessed with genealogy, with ancestors burning in hell because they'd failed to accept the one true religion. If possible, they'd research their forefathers back to Adam so those ancestors could then be raised to heaven during a baptism for the dead.

"My father refused. He said there had to be proof that she had passed on. 'Do it for me,' I begged him. 'Just in case.' But he wouldn't listen."

"Did you keep any of your mother's letters?"

"Only the last few." She dug into her purse again, this time coming up with several envelopes held together by a paper clip. She handed them to Traveler. They smelled of tobacco. All the postmarks were the same, Lydel Springs, Arizona.

"That seems like the logical place to start," he said. "Do you know the name of the group she joined?"

"They call themselves the Church of Zion Reborn."

He quickly read through the letters, finding nothing of interest except a reference to a new husband.

"If she remarried," he said, handing back the stack of correspondence, "she must have divorced your father."

"I think she wrote that just to make Daddy mad. Oh, she was living with a man, all right. My father went on and on about that. Even if she went through some kind of ceremony, my father says it would be illegal."

"Do you know the name of the man she was living with?"

"Oh, yes. It was in one of her letters. His name was Jordan. I remember because it reminded me of the River Jordan right here in Salt Lake, the one named for the original one in the Holy Land."

He emptied the marmalade jar, which no longer smelled fit for pencils.

"What do you think?" she said.

"Before taking a case like this, I like knowing a little more about my subject."

"Talk to my father if you'd like."

"I ought to warn you, sometimes I uncover more than people want to know."

Her head shook as though to deny any such possibility.

"My fee is two hundred and fifty dollars a day, plus expenses."

"How long does it usually take?"

"I've found missing persons in a few hours. Sometimes I never find them."

"A week would take all my savings."

"I'll get back to you before that. Where can I contact you?"

She took five hundred dollars in cash from her wallet along with a business card. "This is my work number. You can reach me here during office hours. I'm on my lunch break right now."

BAPTISM FOR THE DEAD

The card advertised the downtown office of Dr. Jake Ruland, Salt Lake's credit dentist. Medicare accepted. Dentures in a day.

Penny smiled, showing her teeth. "My smile got me the job. I don't have any fillings."

2

By the time she left, snowflakes were spilling from the sky like feathers from some great molting bird. Traveler, his forehead pressed against the cold windowpane, watched her until she turned the next corner at Main Street. Three floors below him on South Temple Street, slush was already beginning to accumulate. Traffic, normally heavy at this time of afternoon, was thinning quickly, as if automobiles knew better than to stay out in one of Utah's April snowstorms.

On the battered wooden table beside him an ancient Philco radio he'd rescued from a garage sale hissed static. Without turning from the window he pounded its green plastic case. The blow produced a spurt of sound; part of a weather forecast calling for continued snow over the next two days, followed by the report of a cult-killing in Bountiful. As soon as static reasserted itself, he pulled the plug.

Laid out on the table adjacent to the radio were the pieces of a fieldstripped M1 rifle from World War II. Each component had been carefully cleaned and oiled.

Even the telescopic sight's metal housing gleamed with lubricant.

He was reaching for the sniper-scope when the phone rang. He picked up the receiver and said, "This is Moroni Traveler."

"Will you please hold for Mr. Willis Tanner," a woman said, her voice curt enough to grate.

"No."

"But . . ."

"If he wants to talk to me, tell him to dial the phone himself."

"Maybe you don't realize who Mr. Tanner is?"

"I do indeed," Traveler said and hung up.

Across the street Mad Bill was circling the temple grounds, his sandwich board a doomed protest in a town dominated by one religion. His placard read REPENT BEFORE IT'S TOO LATE. It was one of several that he rotated on a regular basis.

As always, Mad Bill did his best to look like an Old Testament prophet. His beard was as flowing as his robe, which at the moment was so wet it clung tenaciously to him, turning his gait into a kind of shuffle.

Using the scope, Traveler sighted on his friend, catching him in the cross hairs. Bill chose that moment to peer up at Traveler's window and wave.

"Come inside and dry out," Traveler mouthed, at the same gesturing dramatically to transmit the message. But Bill shook his head and kept moving, holding on to the hem of his garment and the sandwich board at the same time. Finally he stopped to lean against the massive granite wall that surrounded the temple. The stone barrier, like so many aspects of the church, reminded Traveler of a Trojan mentality. But when it came to scaling the walls of Mormonism, Mad Bill was no Agamemnon.

The phone sounded again. Traveler counted half a dozen rings before he picked it up.

"You'll never change," Willis Tanner said immediately.

"Then don't keep trying."

"Will you be there for a while?"

Tanner worked out of the LDS office building two blocks to the east. The structure, a skyscraper by Salt Lake standards, overshadowed even the temple; it also went down into the earth nearly as far as it did into the sky, providing underground storage for church records against the day of Armageddon.

"Look out your window, Willis. It's snowing. Reasonable men would be home sitting in front of a fire."

"That lets us both out then, doesn't it? I'll be in your office in fifteen minutes."

"The last time I worked for you I damn near got killed."

"It's time you joined the church, Moroni. Once you do, you'll realize there are worse things than death."

"I ended up in jail, for God's sake."

"We bailed you out, didn't we?"

"Hire a Mormon in good standing, not a gentile like me."

"You know it's important or I wouldn't be calling."

"Willis, I don't like mixing religion and business. I . . ."

The dial tone cut off further protest.

With a groan Traveler turned his telescopic sight on the temple's highest spire. At the top, a statue of the

Angel Moroni flickered in and out like a figure in a paperweight snowstorm.

Tradition had the statue made of solid gold. But Traveler knew better. It was fourteen-carat plate only and hollow at that.

An escaping breath steamed the windowpane. He wiped away the mist to check the street again. There wasn't a car in sight now. And judging by the way the snow was piling up, only snowplows and lunatics would be moving by nightfall.

On a clear day he could see much of the inner, dying city from his window. Once it had been Brigham Young's glory, a town laid out logically and beautifully, with streets radiating from the center of its life, the temple. The most immediate streets around Brigham's spiritual hub were, quite reasonably, East Temple, North Temple, South Temple, and West Temple. Beyond them lay First North, First West, First East, First South, and so on, all the way out to the city limits. Much of the city had stayed that way for a hundred years, hunkered down in the middle of the prophet's desert sanctuary, guarded by a ring of mountains and the vast lake. Then suddenly the population exploded and, like cancer, grew out to touch the foothills and even the shore, though nature was having something to say about that with the ever-rising waters. Greater Salt Lake, it was called now, with over a million people and everything that went with them.

"Stop thinking so much and go home," Traveler told himself. "You're under no obligation to Tanner."

But Willis was a friend, going all the way back to junior high school. In this case he was also a potential second client; two in one day would be unheard of for a private detective who'd been away from the land of Zion for so many years.

"I'll give you ten minutes, Willis. Starting now."

With that, Traveler began reassembling the rifle. The army had taught him to do it blindfolded. But this time he watched himself work.

The scope was the last piece to lock into place. Once that was done, he fed in a clip of live ammunition. Only then was he satisfied that the weapon was in full working order.

He unloaded the rifle and began stripping it down again, this time with his eyes closed. When he finished, each piece lay on the table in proper order, ready for quick reassembly.

Willis Tanner never seemed to change. He still wore his bright red hair in a crewcut that went all the way back to the eighth grade. His face still screwed itself into a lopsided squint whenever he was under pressure. At the moment, it was completely askew.

"Jesus," Traveler said. "I know that look of yours."

Tanner condemned the blasphemy with a grimace.

"You know me, Willis. A sinner in the land of Zion."

Tanner shook his head sadly and made an obvious effort to relax his face. Then he brushed snow from the shoulders of his overcoat and turned his back as though expecting Traveler to help him out of the garment.

"I'm not one of your wives, Willis."

That brought Tanner whirling around, fists clenched.

He was a high official of the church, sworn to defend it against the slander of polygamy.

Traveler raised his hands in mock surrender. "You wouldn't hit a defenseless gentile, would you?" To a Mormon, all outsiders were gentiles, even Jews.

Tanner was shifting his weight to attack when he slipped on the snow-slick tile underfoot. The bulky overcoat restricted his movements. He had to grab hold of the detective to keep from falling. The office was so small they ended up lurching into a wall.

"I took you once before," Tanner said to cover his embarrassment. "I could do it again."

"That was a long time ago," Traveler said, separating himself from his friend's bear hug. "In those days you had size on me."

Tanner stood up straight as if intending to measure himself against Traveler. Even on tiptoe he couldn't match the other's height.

Frustrated, Tanner took a deep breath to inflate his chest, but still managed to look fragile beside Traveler.

As a troubleshooter for the LDS Church, Willis Tanner wasn't required to use brawn, only his brain. His specialty was public relations. He knew every important journalist from Utah to California and was owed enough favors to suppress anything from heresy to murder, though as far as Traveler knew it had never come to the latter.

"What you need is a drink," Traveler said, meaning it. But his friend took the comment as sacrilege.

"One shot at you," Tanner said. "That's all I ask."

"What do I get in return?"

"Employment."

"I'm not looking for work at the moment."

Tanner sighed. "What am I going to do with you, Moroni? You're my fallen angel."

"I'm named for my father."

Tanner shrugged out of his topcoat and laid it on the client's chair. As usual, he was wearing an expensive, three-piece gray suit. But on him, it looked as if it had come off the rack at Sears. "Your father was named for our angel."

"He didn't ask for it and neither did I."

"Haven't you ever wondered about it? You must have been named Moroni for a reason. Perhaps you're destined to become one of us after all."

"When you start talking like that, Willis, you make me nervous."

Tanner's squint had returned. Sight of it made Traveler squirm inside. In the past Willis had made it through heresy trials without looking troubled in the least. So whatever was bothering him at the moment had to be one hell of a problem.

"I can't help you," Traveler said. "I'm working on something."

"Has Claire been calling you again?"

"Maybe I ought to hire you as a detective."

"Hey, Mo, it's none of my business. But she's been making your life miserable ever since you moved back home."

"I still think of L.A. as home."

"You were born here. That makes you a Utah boy forever."

There was too much truth in that for Traveler to deny it.

"Face it," Tanner went on. "You'll never have any peace until you get Claire Bennion out of your life."

"Maybe she's *my* fallen angel."

"Angels don't get themselves lost all the time and expect private detectives to come find them."

"That's what I do, find people."

"Exactly." Tanner couldn't have looked more pleased if he'd converted Traveler to the Word of Wisdom as pronounced by Joseph Smith.

"All right," Traveler said. "Tell me about it. But I'm not promising anything."

Instead of answering Tanner stepped to the window, cleared a patch in the mist with the palm of his hand, and stared out. After a moment he stepped back just far enough to point, his fingernail tapping the glass. "You're a lucky man having a view like this. The temple, our angel, seeing them both every day."

"I need all the inspiration I can get."

Tanner didn't move. "We've been friends a long time."

Traveler smiled. Between a Mormon and a gentile, true friendship wasn't really possible. He would always be an outsider, even in death. Church doctrine excluded all nonbelievers from salvation. As boys they had been close, before theology got in the way.

"I see you haven't stopped playing with guns," Tanner said, one hand waving vaguely in the M1's direction.

"A man needs a hobby. Besides, this particular gun is part of my past."

Tanner shrugged. "Does the name Varney mean anything to you?" he asked quietly, without turning around.

Traveler grunted to cover his surprise.

"The family goes all the way back to the beginning, Moroni."

"So?"

"The present-day John Varney is a member of the Council of Seventy."

"The question remains. So?"

Tanner slumped as he turned from the window. "He wants you to find his daughter and she's not even missing." He smiled; his good humor looked forced.

"Stop playing games, Willis."

"I don't understand it myself," Tanner said. "They say children are expected to rebel against their parents. But I never did any such thing."

My God, Traveler thought, Willis had a short memory. "I remember you smoking cigarettes with me when we were thirteen years old."

"That's not the same thing."

"The fumes of hell, you told me years later when you were getting ready for your mission."

"Sometimes I think you know me too well, Moroni."

"Come on, Willis. Tell me what you're talking about."

Tanner's squint closed down one eye altogether. "Varney's daughter, Penny, left home a few months ago. Somehow she got it into her head that her father was to blame for her mother's desertion. By the way, the woman ran off and joined one of those crackpot fundamentalist cults." He grimaced like a man taking medicine. To a man like Tanner, fundamentalists were no better than devil-worshipers.

"Which one of them are we talking about?" Traveler asked, feigning ignorance.

"They call themselves the Church of Zion Reborn."

"What's the official line on them?"

Tanner's teeth clenched so hard muscles danced along the line of his jaw. His lips pressed together. He had the look of a man who desperately wanted to swear. What came out of him was a gulping sound, as if he were swallowing sharp-edged obscenities.

Finally he said, "They claim to be the modern-day inheritors of Mormonism. They say our church has strayed from the true teachings of Joseph Smith and Brigham Young. Naturally, they practice polygamy."

"Jesus," Traveler murmured. "Does it never stop, these revelations from God so that horny old men can hump every woman who's willing?" He stared at his boyhood friend and shook his head. Maybe he should have stayed in Los Angeles. There, at least, nothing was sacred except money.

Tanner, his head tilted slightly to one side, had taken on the intense look of a man listening to his own inner voices. "These people don't respect the law. So how can we be expected to stop them?"

Traveler said nothing, but knew it wasn't as simple as that. The church had influence enough to stop just about anybody or anything if it had a mind to. But when it came to polygamy, doctrine wasn't all that clear. A century ago pragmatism and a federal army had put an official end to multiple wives. But to this day, there were still those who followed Joseph Smith's revelation, prefaced as it was by words that gave no leeway. *For behold, I reveal unto you a new and everlasting covenant; and if ye abide not that covenant, then ye are damned; for no one can reject this covenant and be permitted to enter into my glory.*

"Church policy is strictly hands-off," Tanner went on. "Officially, we don't even recognize these people."

"I still don't understand what this has to do with Penny."

Tanner sat heavily on top of his damp overcoat. His eyes looked everywhere but at Traveler. His words, when they came, sounded rehearsed. " 'Suppose you found your brother in bed with your wife, and put a javelin through both of them, you would be justified, and they would atone for their sins and be received into the kingdom of God.' " He gulped a breath. "Brigham Young wrote that."

"You're talking blood atonement."

Tanner nodded like a man whose head worked independently of his body. "There has been a lot of bloodletting in these cults over the past few years. This morning we had another killing, just outside the city limits in Bountiful. The dead man's name was Jordan. Earl Jordan. He belonged to the Church of Zion Reborn."

"Goddammit, Willis, have you got a bug in here?"

"What are you talking about?"

"Penny Varney was here less than a half hour ago. The name Jordan came up in the conversation. You wouldn't be here if you didn't know that already."

"When these cults start killing one another a lot of blood gets spilled."

"Penny's mother?"

"We have no information on her at the moment."

Traveler moved to the window, used one finger to rub a peephole in the mist, and peered toward the temple. But there was only swirling snow to be seen. He leaned forward and breathed on the glass until the

28

hole disappeared. "My understanding is that the Church of Zion Reborn is headquartered in Arizona."

"Hey, Mo. We have to root out heresy wherever it exists."

"That sounds suspiciously like you had the man killed yourself."

"I do God's work, nothing else."

"Out," Traveler said, pointing at the door. "I'm hungry and I want to go home."

"Don't get excited. There's more to tell. John Varney wants to hire you to keep an eye on his daughter. If you can convince her to come back home, he'll pay a handsome bonus."

"I see. I watch the girl and you watch me, is that it?"

"He hasn't seen his daughter in months. Think of it as a missing person case."

"As you well know, I already have a client."

"If it wasn't for this murder, we wouldn't care what the girl did. As it is, the church has no choice but to get involved."

Traveler bent down to stare at his friend. Not exactly a friend, he reminded himself. This was church business now. A gentile was wanted, perhaps as a sacrifice. He straightened. "Spell it out, Willis. I want to know exactly what I'm expected to do."

"That's easy. Protect our interests. Keep Penny Varney and her mother out of the papers. We don't want them connected with the likes of Earl Jordan."

"Bullshit. You own most of the papers. Those you don't will look the other way if you ask them to."

"There are always wire-service stringers to contend with. You can't trust journalists." Tanner kneaded his face as if he were trying to remold it into something less revealing. "We want you on Penny's case, not the police. At least not officially."

"There's already been a murder, for God's sake. Besides, you own the police, too."

"You never know when one of them might get religion."

Traveler blinked. "I think you made a joke, Willis."

Tanner shook his head as if to deny it. Then he took a quick breath and said, "We've already gone ahead and arranged a contact for you at the police department, Lieutenant Anson Horne. He's been instructed to give you whatever help you might need."

"We?"

"Elton Woolley is taking a personal interest in this."

Traveler pretended to examine his disassembled rifle. Automatically his hands busied themselves applying another coat of oil to the M1's trigger housing.

Elton Woolley was president of the Mormon Church. To believers, he was the living prophet on earth. Through him, as it had been with Joseph Smith in the beginning, came the word of God. Without question, Woolley was the most powerful man in the State of Utah. He could make life impossible for someone like Traveler.

"You do this for us," Tanner said, "and you'll never lack for work in this town."

"Give it a rest," Traveler said and gave up his charade of working on the M1. He wiped his hands carefully on a paper towel, but the smell of gun oil remained.

"I have a copy of the police report on the killing." Tanner dug an envelope from his inside coat pocket and held it out like an offering. "You're seeing this before it reaches the chief's office."

Traveler grunted appreciatively. The murder couldn't have been more than a few hours old.

He didn't bother reading the Xeroxed sheets. "All right. Tell me what's been left out of the news reports."

Abruptly the squint left Tanner's face. So did all color. He swallowed noticeably. "The girl can't be involved in this, Moroni."

"You'd better explain that."

Tanner squirmed in his chair as though suddenly realizing that he was sitting on his wet overcoat. Then he sprang to his feet and stepped quickly to the window, where he feigned looking out without even bothering to clear a hole in the mist.

"Someone saw a girl leaving the scene. A blond girl."

"Salt Lake is known for its blondes."

"Martha Varney used to be a blonde." From his wallet Tanner produced a small snapshot. "She was much younger then, of course."

"I thought I was supposed to be keeping an eye on Penny Varney."

Compressed into a one-by-one-inch square, Martha Varney looked different from her daughter's larger photograph. This time she had light hair and wasn't smiling.

"Is she a natural blonde?"

"As far as I know." Tanner clicked his tongue. "She doesn't look like that anymore, I'm told."

31

Traveler turned the photograph over in his hand. A twenty-year-old date was penciled on the back. "What good is this going to do me, then?"

"Elton Woolley thought you ought to have it, that's all."

"I don't believe he even knows my name." He sure as hell hoped not.

"Our prophet keeps track of all Moronis."

"Sure. Angels all. Now tell me, is there anything else you haven't mentioned?"

"You'll do better talking to John Varney." Tanner extracted one of his calling cards from an expensive-looking leather holder. "His address and phone number are on the back. He's expecting you within the hour."

"Were you that sure of me, Willis?"

"I've known you a long time, Mo."

"I've raised my rates."

Tanner raised an eyebrow. "We'll cover any legitimate costs."

"If I agree, I'd want something in advance."

"Like I said, I've known you a long time." Tanner counted out two thousand dollars in one-hundred-dollar bills.

"The girl comes first. If I can find her mother and keep an eye on her at the same time, fine. Otherwise, it's no deal. I'm not spending a dime of your money either, not until I find all the strings you've attached."

"John Varney's the one you answer to."

"Not Elton Woolley?"

Tanner slipped into his overcoat.

"I'll give you a receipt."

"No, no," Tanner said, backing away. "We don't want anything in writing. The church isn't involved in this. You haven't even seen me."

"You know something, Willis? I'm already beginning to wish I hadn't."

3

Traveler stepped out of the elevator and into a lobby reeking of Mormon hellfire. Satan's work had been done by generations of smokers who'd paused at the cigar stand to light up their sins.

The stand itself was sandwiched between two massive Doric columns of marble that held up one corner of the lobby. The stand's glass-topped display case was like something from a time warp, filled with pouches of Bull Durham, cigarette papers, Chiclets, and Sen-Sen. There was even a perpetual gas flame for the convenience of smokers.

The man behind the counter, Barney Chester, had his head craned back, staring at the ceiling. Traveler glanced up, too, enjoying the depression-era frescoes that depicted the pioneers pulling handcarts along the Mormon Trail. Leading the trek was Brigham Young.

"Cigarette smoke is turning him yellow," Chester observed as soon as Traveler came within earshot. "Every goddamned day he looks a little more jaundiced."

Traveler leaned back to squint at Brigham one more time. "You could always have the ceiling cleaned."

"You don't touch works of art like that. Not these days. Not with artists painting shit that looks like something a dog wouldn't piss on." Chester liked talking tough. He thought it went along with his image, because someone had once told him that he looked like Edward G. Robinson portraying a gangster.

"A little soap and water is all I'm suggesting."

"My ceiling goes back to the thirties, for Christ's sake. In those days artists worked out of love."

"Three meals a day was more like it."

"You'll never convince me of that."

Such conversations had become a ritual between them. The words changed from day to day, but never the camaraderie they generated.

"There's only one other choice then," Traveler said. "Put up no-smoking signs."

"I'll let Brigham turn black first."

To prove his point, Chester lit a cigar, drew in a lungful of smoke, and then fired it toward the ceiling. If Barney Chester hadn't been the landlord, both he and his stand would have been memories long ago. There was nothing Mormons hated more than smoking.

"How about something to read?" he asked.

This, too, was ritual.

As always Traveler refused to take the bait, though he knew full well that Barney kept salacious paperbacks and antichurch literature under the counter as temptations for his friends. He would never offer them to anyone who might be offended.

"In case you haven't noticed," Traveler said, "it's snowing outside."

"And Bill?"

35

"Walking his beat as usual."

"Do me a favor, Moroni. Get him to come inside. He listens to you." Chester nodded at a shiny new coffee maker that stood next to a cash register as old as the frescoes overhead. "Tell him I've got hot coffee and doughnuts."

Traveler leaned over to peer behind the counter. As usual Bill's sleeping bag was rolled up and stashed in the corner out of sight of the customers. Next to it stood a bedroll belonging to a Navajo named Charlie Redwine.

"You're too soft to be a landlord," Traveler said, pushing himself away from the display case.

In response Chester clamped tobacco-stained teeth around his cigar and said, "Oh, yeah?" It almost made him sound like Edward G. Robinson.

"You want me to get Charlie in here, too?"

"Why the hell not? At least when it's this cold they don't smell so bad."

"You keep this up, and you won't have any tenants left."

"Bullshit. Where else are you going to find rents this low, not to mention a view that would make a prophet proud? Answer me that, will ya?"

Traveler couldn't. Most of Salt Lake's grand old buildings had been torn down to make way for shopping malls.

"Tell Bill if he gets pneumonia I'm not going to nurse him. And I'm not buying any more wine for that Indian, either."

Traveler shook his head but said nothing. He knew there was always a half-gallon jug of dago red under the counter along with the paperback pornography.

"And tell them to wipe their feet before they come in here," Chester added.

"Some of us have real work to do," Traveler said. "We don't have time for errands."

"Since when?"

"I've had two clients today. The last one just left."

"*Him*, I saw. You don't need funny business like that."

"It pays the rent."

"In weather like this, it's better you should stay inside and keep dry." Chester had given up on Edward G. Robinson to become a Jewish mother.

"I'll get Bill." Traveler headed for the revolving door made of panels of art deco bronze and glass, the last of its kind in town.

Outside, snow was falling with such intensity that the temple had become a soft shadow, its spires no more than tantalizing images at the edge of memory. The Angel Moroni had been erased altogether.

Traveler caught movement near one of the temple gates. He cupped his hands beside his mouth and shouted, "Bill, come inside."

A gust of wind blew snow in Traveler's face. Along with it came the shouted reply, "The Lord be praised."

Then Mad Bill came as fast as he could, the sandwich board banging his shins with each step. He was a big man, about equal in bulk to Traveler, but with most of his weight arranged around his middle.

"I've been praying for sunshine," Bill said as soon as he joined Traveler in front of the Chester Building. "Your call was God's way of answering me, telling me that my work was done for the day and that I could come in out of the cold."

Traveler had been prepared for a long argument, since Bill was usually reluctant to leave his post.

Bill pointed a finger at the heavens. "This weather is a sign. I know it."

"Where's Charlie?" Traveler asked to forestall any preaching.

"Down the street at the Era Antiques."

"Selling or stealing?"

"Charlie doesn't have anything to sell. What he gets, the Lord provides."

Traveler, hunching his shoulders in a vain attempt to keep snowflakes from sliding down his neck, grabbed hold of the sandwich prophet, as Bill liked to call himself, and pulled them both under cover of the building's overhang. "Bill, you're soaked clear through."

"I answer God's call."

"What does He say about overcoats?"

Bill ignored the comment to concentrate on freeing himself from the sandwich boards. But at the moment, chilblained fingers made such a maneuver impossible.

With a grunt, Traveler tugged the plywood placards over his friend's head. Once free of them, Bill led the way inside where he immediately attempted to use the hem of his robe to dry his signs. The woolen material was too sodden to be of any use.

Traveler donated his handkerchief to the cause. "Maybe I ought to go get Charlie?"

"If he doesn't get picked up for shoplifting, he'll be here any minute."

As if on cue the Indian pushed through the revolving door.

Bill leaned his boards against the nearest wall, then opened his arms and said, "Charlie, what has God bestowed upon us?"

The Navajo, who had spent two years studying anthropology at Brigham Young University before peyote intervened, held up one hand like a movie Indian and replied, "How." It was just about all he ever said. Traveler suspected it was Charlie's way of laughing at them.

Then he extended his hand. It held a beaded necklace of lapis lazuli.

"Ah," said Mad Bill, palming the offering. "I have just the parishioner for this." He tucked the jewelry into a Levi pocket beneath his robe.

Charlie nodded, his face as stoic as the proverbial wooden Indian, and started toward the cigar stand.

Traveler nudged one of Bill's sandwich boards with his shoe and read, "Repent before it's too late."

"I'm through with those for today," Bill responded, following the Indian. "Tomorrow we move on to 'God is love.' "

"One of these days," Traveler said, "you're going to get yourself arrested."

"The Lord will protect me."

"And Charlie?"

"He has the Bureau of Indian Affairs."

Barney Chester had plastic cups of hot coffee on the display case. The Hostess doughnuts were so old they had to be dunked.

As Traveler concentrated on keeping his pastry submerged, Barney nodded at Mad Bill and said, "Our

39

friend Moroni has just been called upon by the church.''

''*The* church,'' Bill repeated. ''That's all I ever hear in this town. Not my church, your church, our church, only *the* church.''

''And why not?'' said Barney. ''After all, you're an institution, too. People call you *the* sandwich prophet.''

''They'll call me more than that one day.''

''Don't get Bill started,'' Traveler said.

''Started?'' Bill mocked. ''I've never stopped. For 'sandwich prophet' substitute 'true prophet.' Take a look outside. The end is near just as I've been predicting. Snow in April is a message from God.''

''Maybe that's why the church wants our Moroni working for them.''

''Why should they?'' Bill answered. ''They're responsible for what's happening.''

''Here it comes,'' Traveler said.

Barney said, ''I read somewhere that there's unusual weather all over the world.''

''It's God's will,'' Bill said.

''Maybe *He's* after the church,'' Barney put in. ''All this moisture is raising hell with the Great Salt Lake. The damn thing's already higher than any time in recorded history. It won't be long before Brigham Young's promised land is under water.''

Bill forgot about the doughnut in his hand and scratched his head, causing crumbs to shower down on his shoulders. ''Nuclear testing?'' he whispered, as if trying out a new theory. ''That could be causing it, but only if the church is behind it.''

''You might as well say the Russians are responsible," Barney said. He pointed a finger at the Indian. "What do you think?"

Charlie's only answer was to stuff another doughnut into his crumb-thickened coffee.

"It's closer to home than the Russians," Bill said. "It's another one of those damned conspiracies. The church owns the FBI, maybe even the CIA."

At times like this Traveler couldn't help wondering if Mad Bill wasn't living up to his name. But sane or not, he did know a great deal about the religious forces opposing him.

"Tell me what you know about the Church of Zion Reborn," Traveler said.

"Enough to stay away from them. Those people are obsessed with bloodletting. To them, murder is a good deed. They think their victims should be thankful to their killers for setting them free of sin."

"Have you ever been among them?"

"Is that why the church has called upon you?" Bill asked.

Traveler shrugged but Bill wasn't fooled. "Stay away from them, Moroni. I tell you that as a friend."

4

By the time Traveler reached the parking lot two blocks away, his car looked like a white burial mound. He hadn't thought to wear gloves when the day began, so he tucked his hands inside his coat sleeves and started wiping away the snow with his arms. Even so his fingers went numb as soon as he opened the trunk and touched the frigid tire chains. For a moment he thought about driving off without them. But there was absolutely no traffic on the road now, no ruts in which to follow. He'd have to blaze his own trail. And he knew better than to try that without chains.

Fitting them took thirty minutes thanks to balky fingers and a wind that half blinded him with snow. By the time Traveler started the engine, his coat was soaked through. Enough snow had melted down his neck to dampen his shirt and underwear. If he could keep his car on the road, he'd have just enough time to make his appointment with John Varney.

But he was in no condition to work at the moment. What he needed was some hot food, something more substantial than Barney's doughnut.

The windshield wipers had a hard time keeping up

as he drove the four blocks to Third South, where he parked in front of Duffy's, a rib joint that had once been called The Zang, a hangout of his youth. Despite the blizzard, the place was packed, a mixture of those like himself there for the nostalgia and a younger generation raised on TV dinners who didn't know any better than to eat the food.

He ordered *The Southern Delight*, pork ribs, cole slaw, and corn bread and honey, more than enough calories to keep up his body temperature.

"You want a beer to go with that?" asked Duffy, a thin man who drank nothing but milk because of an ulcer. His face was so shiny it looked like he was sweating rib fat.

"Better not," said Traveler, thinking what effect beer fumes might have on a man like John Varney. "Give me some coffee to cut the grease."

Duffy hugged himself and made a show of shuddering. "Do you know what this crap does to your stomach?"

"Why do you sell it, then?"

"Because I'm too poor to afford a McDonald's franchise."

"Speaking of poverty, how do I stand on credit?"

Duffy raised a damp eyebrow. "How much do you need?"

"Just tell me the score."

With a shake of his head, Duffy limped over to the cash register and ruffled through a stack of chits that were pinned to a spindle. "Not counting what you eat today, there's another fifty left in your bank."

Traveler suspected that amount was too high, but he said nothing. It made Duffy feel good to have a way of paying him back for investigating his wife's love life, something Traveler wouldn't have done for anyone but a friend.

Next to the spindle holding credits stood another sharp spike for IOUs. Messages, however, were taped to a mirror behind the cash register.

"I got a call for you earlier," Duffy said, not turning around, but eyeing Traveler in the glass. He pulled a note from his reflection and handed it over his shoulder. "It's from Claire."

The note said: *I'm lost. Find me.*

She made a game of leaving messages at all his favorite haunts. Some of them were embarrassing.

A bell rang in the kitchen. Instantly Duffy headed for the swinging door, moving at a fast hop like a man who'd been waiting for any excuse to get away. His limp, the result of trying to bounce one too many drunks, made him look like a man dodging invisible obstacles.

The door flapped behind him. But almost immediately he reappeared, looking sheepish and bearing Traveler's order.

"Did she say anything else?" Traveler asked as soon as the man set down the plate.

"Not for you. But she sent Mad Bill her love."

Traveler snagged a sparerib and pretended to enjoy it. But it was Claire he was thinking about, and Bill, who had once offered to give up his sandwich boards for her. His offer, like Traveler's love, had sparked her scorn.

Traveler and Claire hadn't been living together more than a week before she disappeared the first time.

44

After three days of frantic searching, hospitals, police, the morgue, the first of her collect calls came in.

"I was so happy I had to leave," she'd explained. "You know the feeling, Moroni. Get away while things are still good, before it all turns sour. But this was a mistake. I shouldn't have come here. I'm in trouble."

"Where are you?"

"I need money."

"Tell me where to send it."

"He wants you to deliver it in person."

"Who does?"

"He says he'll sell me to a bunch of drunken Indians if you don't bring it."

"White slavery has been dead a long time, Claire."

"Please, honey. There are Indians here. Really."

As if on cue he heard chanting in the background.

"Where are you?" he asked again.

"Out in the middle of nowhere."

"Tell me."

"He said he'd hurt me if I did."

"We can't play Twenty Questions. I can't bring the money if I don't know where you are."

"Oh, that's right. I'll have to ask him."

Traveler heard voices for a moment, then someone must have clamped a hand over the receiver.

At last she said, "It's a roadhouse named Bonnie and Ben's Bonanza. It's out on State Highway Thirty-three between Duchesne and Castle Gate. You can't miss the place. It's on the east side of the road just after you leave the Indian reservation."

"Who gets the money?"

There was a pause before she said, "Ben does."

"How much does he want?"

"Five hundred."

The Uintah and Ouray Reservation was a tough drive even in daylight. At night it took four hours to negotiate the one hundred and twenty miles. By the time Traveler got there, it was nearly two o'clock in the morning.

Once parked, he removed his pistol from its shoulder holster and checked the clip. Then he unlocked the car door and stepped out onto the gravel parking area.

Bonnie and Ben's Bonanza looked like a lean-to that had been dragged far enough off the reservation to make free enterprise legal. The floor was covered with gritty sawdust that crunched underfoot. The bar, faced by half a dozen rickety-looking wooden stools, was nothing more than a long plank resting on top of four large wooden barrels.

Only one stool was occupied, and that was by Claire. Indians and men dressed like cowboys stood around her in a semicircle, teetering on their high-heeled boots and vying to buy drinks. Even the bartender, a middle-aged man with a glistening bald head and beer belly the size of a keg, was out from behind his countertop.

Claire didn't notice Traveler's arrival, but the bartender did.

"I'm looking for Ben," Traveler said.

"You've found him."

Traveler hadn't thought about it beforehand, hadn't decided on a plan of action. In fact, for a split second he didn't realize what he'd done. Then he felt the pain in his fist and saw Ben crashing headfirst into one of the wooden barrels. But that didn't stop Traveler from hauling the man back onto his feet and hitting him again. Bone crunched.

In the end it took both Indians and cowboys to pull him off the battered bartender.

Finally, Claire's voice penetrated Traveler's blazing anger. "It was only a game, Moroni. I had to know if you loved me enough to come save me."

He blinked. His eyes glazed over. His muscles went slack. His arms fell to his sides.

After that, the Indians worked him over with impunity. Finally they got tired of beating on a man who wouldn't fight back and threw him out. Claire followed a moment later, grabbing Traveler's car keys and getting them out of there as fast as she could.

They stayed the night at a motel in the small farming town of Helper. In the morning Traveler, without identifying himself, called the Bonanza to check on Ben. He was in the hospital, Bonnie reported, listed in fair condition. As an afterthought, Traveler said he was a reporter and asked for the address. A few minutes later he mailed the five hundred in ransom money he'd brought with him to the Bonanza.

The next time Claire disappeared, she made the game harder, refusing to give him any location at all. He found her after a long search, but then moved out of her place and back home with his father. He'd intended to go apartment hunting immediately but somehow hadn't gotten around to it yet.

"Well?" Duffy said. "How are the ribs?"

Traveler swallowed his mouthful. "If Bill comes around looking for handouts, put it on my tab."

"Charlie, too?"

Traveler nodded.

"That's fine with me, as long as you understand they have to order it to go. I can't have them in here killin' the smell of my ribs."

"Un-hunh," Traveler said. "I don't think anything could do that." He spun off his stool and headed for the telephone at the back of the café.

After wiping barbecue sauce from his hands, he dialed the number given to him by Willis Tanner.

A woman answered, "Varney residence."

"This is Moroni Traveler. Mr. Varney is expecting me."

"I'll see if he's in," came her cold reply.

A moment later a deep, commanding voice said, "Where are you, Mr. Traveler?"

"I'm going to be late."

"Is there a problem with the weather?"

Only if you're out in it, he was tempted to say. "I won't be there for another hour at least."

"The forecast calls for this storm to get worse before it gets better," Varney said. "We live up near the mountains. Maybe you won't be able to get here at all."

"I'll be with you as soon as I can." Traveler paused, waiting for further comment. But none came, only the dial tone.

By the time Traveler returned to his stool, his spareribs had cooled, crusting with fat. The sight killed his appetite.

He left a dollar tip and walked outside, where visibility was down to a few yards. Walking was probably a lot safer than driving, but his next stop, the library, was too far away for a man without boots.

Childhood memory led him momentarily astray as he turned north on State Street, heading for the old Carnegie-funded library, a sculptured sandstone delight. But that had long since given way to a characterless repository on Second East and Fifth South.

Beneath white flourescent lights that washed all signs of humanity from every face, he found what he was looking for—biographical data on John Varney.

The man was forty-two years old, married to Martha Ann Snow, and had one daughter, Penelope—unusual for an official of a church whose doctrine demanded large families. Varney was also considered to be one of Mormonism's leading theological writers, the author of several books on genealogy, including one on baptism for the dead. Traveler checked that one out and carried it to an empty reading table, where he skimmed it quickly. The volume, though published at church expense, seemed to be aimed at nonbelievers. It explained the Mormon obsession with ancestor research, that those born before Joseph Smith revealed the true church could be raised to heaven only by baptism in absentia. All other gentiles would be damned to hell.

Such baptisms for the dead, Traveler knew, far outnumbered those for the living.

He returned the heavy volume to its proper shelf and then got help from a pasty-faced librarian who provided him with several microfilmed clippings dealing with the Church of Zion Reborn. A report in *Time* magazine mentioned the group only in passing, concentrating on the fact that southern Utah and northern Arizona were hotbeds of offshoot religious cults, most stemming from Mormonism. Many of them had been forced underground by law enforcement agencies and other, more reckless, sects. One informant, who refused to be named because he feared for his life, said the goal of these sects was to undermine the Mormon Church from within.

Another national publication pinpointed the Church of Zion Reborn near the small Arizona community of Lydel Springs, where several unsolved killings had taken place over the last few years. The local sheriff was quoted as saying the circumstances surrounding the murders had been bizarre. He suspected some kind of blood ritual.

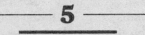

5

The Varney estate spread over several acres of Federal Heights, an older section in the foothills northeast of town. The house itself, situated at the top of Arlington Drive, was two stories of bleached brick that looked as if life had drained away right along with the color.

Federal Heights had taken its name from nearby government land on which Fort Douglas had been built. Some said the fortification had been placed in the foothills, commanding the high ground, as a reminder to nineteenth-century Mormons that they had to follow the nation's rules like everyone else. Whatever the case, much of the area was still populated by wealthy gentiles, whose pioneering families, well aware of Brigham Young's Mountain Meadow Massacre, thought it wise to stick close to more traditional law and order. It was a strange neighborhood to find a family that traced its roots back to Joseph Smith's days in Nauvoo.

As a precaution against drifting snow, Traveler maneuvered his Ford carefully until it was pointing downhill. Only then did he make the hike to the front door.

51

Pausing, he looked up at the clouds. For a moment, there was only swirling snow to be seen. Then, almost without transition, the flakes dissipated, revealing bright sky. Perhaps he was standing in the eye of the storm, or maybe it was only a freak opening in the front, but suddenly the clouds parted even more, exposing the surrounding mountains. For decades those sharp granite pinnacles had served as Brigham Young's fortress against his enemies in the east, better than any man-made citadel.

The sky closed, swallowing both sky and mountains. Traveler hunched his shoulders and knocked on the door.

The woman who greeted him had a face as bleak as the brick exterior. She wore no makeup. Her eyes were the watery blue of melting ice. Her silvery-blond hair was pulled back so tightly into a bun that it looked as if it had been lacquered in place.

She was dressed entirely in gray, with a heavy pleated skirt that caught her at midcalf, a gray pullover sweater, and on top of that a cable-stitched cardigan that hid any sign of breasts.

Her bloodless lips tightened to a grim white line before she said, "Mr. Traveler?"

He nodded.

She didn't invite him in, but merely stepped to one side clearing the way for him. He moved past her into an entrance hall that reminded him of an old Gothic movie. It had a suit of armor holding a broadsword, a coat of arms on the wall, and a circular staircase leading to the bedrooms upstairs. At any moment he expected to see Joan Fontaine sweeping down to receive him.

Standing beneath a crystal chandelier, Traveler brushed enough snow from his hair and raincoat to create slush underfoot.

"Sorry for the mess. It looked like spring just this morning."

She answered with a smile so brief it could have been a figment of his imagination. Then, with the slightest sigh, she reached for a light switch next to the door. Bright shivers of light radiated from a hundred crystals. Some of the sharp rays highlighted her face, revealing red-rimmed eyes that suggested she'd been crying. He could also see that she was much younger than he'd thought at first. Forty, he estimated. Maybe a little less. About the right age to be Penny's mother, only she had to be the aunt. There was a definite family resemblance, with a trace of the girl's beauty, but carefully hidden as if it were some terrible burden.

"Mrs. . . . ?" he said.

"Mrs. Varney is dead," she answered. Her terminology made him wonder what she knew that he didn't. "I'm the housekeeper."

She made no move, but stood staring at him as if he were some kind of alien species.

"John Varney is expecting me," he prompted.

She nodded and crossed the entrance hall, pausing before a massive oak door. Her knock was timid, but the door jerked open immediately as if someone on the other side had been awaiting her prearranged signal.

A hand was thrust across the threshold toward Traveler. He grasped it, surprised by the strength in the long, thin fingers. Then the rest of the man came into view, a lean figure with dark red hair and mustache to match. But on closer inspection, his leanness did not extend to his stomach, which protruded over a tightly cinched belt. He reminded Traveler of a snake that had swallowed its prey whole.

"Thank God you've come. I'm John Varney."

He shook hands again as if the mention of his name required an additional commitment.

"You're cold," Varney said, rubbing his own fingers in sympathy. "Would you like a drink?"

Surprise must have shown in Traveler's face, because Varney smiled and said, "Will Tanner told me you were a nonbeliever. But I see you have some knowledge of us." He closed his eyes briefly. When he spoke again he did so like an actor reciting lines. " 'Hot drinks are not for the body or belly.' " He paused, eyeing Traveler expectantly. "Do you recognize the words?"

"Joseph Smith."

"Excellent. There's hope for you yet."

Traveler shrugged. The quote was part of the church's doctrine and covenants outlawing alcohol, tobacco, and even coffee and tea. More commonly these strictures were known as the Word of Wisdom.

Behind him the housekeeper sniffed derisively.

"Two cups of hot milk," Varney told her, his tone a dismissal.

She left without a word of acknowledgment.

"Pearl has a secret recipe. She adds a little vanilla and sugar to her concoction."

Traveler refrained from pointing out that vanilla contained alcohol. A sin was a sin only when you knew about it.

Now that they were alone Varney looked somewhat embarrassed. Most people did when they called in a private detective.

To give the man time to recover, Traveler turned away to study the room. Walnut bookshelves covered all four walls from baseboard to ceiling, except for a French door opening out onto a stand of aspen. Every inch of shelving was crammed with impressive-looking volumes.

Traveler selected one of the more elaborately bound books, done in red Moroccan leather with gold embossing. It was one of Varney's own, *Genes and Genealogy*. There was not so much as a speck of dust on it.

The volume felt virginal so he replaced it quickly and turned to face Varney, who was now seated behind an antique partners' desk. Traveler took the facing chair, his legs jammed into a footwall designed in an era when people were smaller. His hands rested on the dark green leather desktop.

"Well," Varney began, his expression suddenly anxious, "did Will Tanner brief you about this business in Bountiful?"

Traveler nodded.

"I know my daughter, Mr. Traveler. She can't be involved in anything like murder." He closed his eyes. "I quote from our good book. 'I must needs destroy the secret works of darkness, and of murders, and of abominations.' "

"It's your wife I'm looking for, Mr. Varney, as I'm sure Willis Tanner told you."

Varney's eyes opened and looked away. "Penny has become obsessed on that subject."

"I wouldn't call a daughter's love for her mother an obsession."

"They weren't actually married, you know," Varney said hastily. "Martha and that man who was killed."

Traveler said nothing.

"Not in God's eyes, anyway." Varney held out his hands, palms up in a gesture of resignation. "I suppose even cult people conduct some sort of pagan ritual. Such marriages can't be legal, not in civil law and certainly not in canon law."

He caught his breath. "If people are to read my books and believe, I must set them an example. I must be beyond reproach. So should my family."

"I seem to remember original sin going from father to son, not wife to husband."

"The saints believe that men will be punished for their own sins, not Adam's. But that's God's punishment. Here on earth we have to worry about appearances."

Traveler leaned forward across the desktop and locked eyes with Varney. It annoyed him that Mormons called one another saints, as if they had to constantly reassure one another of their piety. "Tell me about your wife," he said.

"We're hiring you to keep an eye on my daughter. Didn't Willis tell you?"

"I'm a free agent, Mr. Varney."

The man leapt to his feet and began examining the books directly behind him. After a moment, he selected a volume, briefly caressed its binding, then began thumbing through it. Occasionally he nodded as if encountering a favorite passage. Finally, his fingers began tapping insistently on one particular page. He nodded to himself and turned to face Traveler.

"The one true book," he said, stepping forward to wave the volume in Traveler's face. *The Book of Mormon.*"

Abruptly he straightened his shoulders, gulped a quick breath, and read, " 'And it shall come to pass, they that are left in Zion and remain in Jerusalem shall be called holy, every one that is written among the living in Jerusalem, when the Lord shall have washed away the filth of the daughters of Zion. . . .' "

For an instant he held the book out toward Traveler before dramatically snapping it shut. "My wife is unclean."

"And your daughter?"

Varney tilted his head to one side as if listening to the question echo inside his mind. Then he sat down again, placing the book on the desk in front of him, his left hand resting on top of it like a witness about to swear to the truth of his testimony.

"Perhaps it's my fault," he said, twitching as if suddenly chilled. "This all seems like a nightmare that keeps repeating itself. First Martha left me, and now Penny." He sighed. "I tried to raise my daughter the best I knew how, but it wasn't enough. I've never been good with children."

"You could have remarried."

He rubbed his face with both hands. "Martha and I were not married in the temple. If we had been, we would be bound together for eternity."

Traveler thought of being bound to Claire in the Mormon way. He shook his head. One lifetime was more than enough with most women.

Varney misinterpreted the gesture. "I assure you, Mr. Traveler, I am not a man to shed a wife as a matter of convenience. I do not believe in divorce, though I realize that times have forced the church to become more liberal. I've never filed the necessary legal documents to free myself of Martha. Whether or not she has done so, I don't know. Certainly I've never been served with any kind of divorce papers."

"I don't deal in consciences, Mr. Varney. Just tell me something about your wife that might help me find her."

For a moment Varney looked as if he were about to object. Then, nodding, he said, "Martha lacked faith. I knew that when I married her but I thought I could show her the way. When that didn't work I gave up to concentrate on Penny. My daughter had to believe. Anything else was unthinkable. But now?" He spread his arms as though seeking someone to hold. "Penny got away from me somehow. Her sin is mine. Mine and Martha's."

"I got the idea from your housekeeper that your wife is dead."

"That's my sister, Pearl, speaking. I don't have a housekeeper. She thinks I ought to have one, though. She says it befits a man in my position. I brought Pearl here to live with us when I realized how much Penny needed a woman around. But an aunt's not the same as a mother, I'm afraid."

"Your daughter thinks something might have happened to her mother."

"I don't know. There was a time when Penny's faith was so strong that she became terrified her mother might die without being baptized into the church. I tried telling her that Martha wouldn't want any such thing. But Penny wouldn't listen. She said she couldn't face eternity without her mother. Even as young as Penny was at the time, it was blasphemy for her to say such a thing. She begged me to perform a baptism for the dead. But we had no proof that Martha had passed over. As for the living, they have to find their own way to the true church.''

Varney slammed his open hand down on *The Book of Mormon*. Veins stood out on his thin neck. His skin seemed to flatten against his face, and for a moment Traveler had the impression that he could see the man's skull showing through. The illusion faded as soon as Varney spoke again. ''Was it my faith or Penny's that failed?''

''I don't give absolution either,'' Traveler said, wondering what the hell he was doing there. A woman had been missing from this house for five years. On top of that a murder had been committed, probably in the name of God, something better left to the police, or perhaps an exorcist. Certainly not a private detective.

Varney looked startled. ''I don't mean to sound sorry for myself. Penny is my problem. At least she will be if you can convince her to come back to me.''

''I find people. Your daughter is not exactly lost.''

''As for Martha,'' Varney went on as though deaf, ''I don't know whether she's alive or dead. And frankly, I'm not certain that I care anymore, except for Penny's sake. You have to understand Martha. Her desertion was carefully planned to hurt me and my career. Why else would she have taken up with polygamists in the desert?''

His head shook slowly from side to side. ''I should

59

have seen it coming. I should have realized that Penny would go off looking for her mother."

"What do you know about Earl Jordan's killing?"

"The police informed me about it, of course. Other than that, I don't know the details. I didn't ask for any."

Traveler stared, wondering if that was the truth. "Penny tells me her mother stopped writing to her about six months ago."

"More like a year. I'd held back some of her letters. When more stopped coming, I parceled out those I'd accumulated to Penny one at a time. Six months ago I ran out." He chewed at his lower lip. "Whatever else Martha is, she was a good mother. It's not like her to stop writing."

"What do you think happened?"

"I wish I knew, Mr. Traveler."

"I understand Penny called the sheriff in Lydel Springs."

"That's right. All Martha's letters were postmarked from there."

"Penny showed me some of those letters. Do you have any more?"

"There might be some in my daughter's room."

"May I take a look?"

"Of course. I'll show you myself." Varney led the way, *The Book of Mormon* clutched to his chest like an amulet against evil.

Penny's room was done in white, white walls, white carpet, white curtains, white furniture. The lack of color made her collection of teddy bears look all the more cheerful. They lined three windowsills; they sat in a careful row atop a vanity table; they lounged on a writing desk; they marched across the pillows at the head of her bed.

"This is just the way my daughter left it," Varney said.

"She must be a very tidy young lady."

"My sister insists. She says you never know when we might have company."

Traveler opened both closets. Clothes were displayed as precisely as the bears.

"Does she ever come home to change?"

"You'd have to ask my sister about that."

Traveler checked the desk. Its middle drawer was divided into neat compartments, one filled with pencils, another paper clips, and still another with erasers. At the rear of the drawer he found a well-worn address book.

He thumbed through it quickly. Two names were on the flyleaf, Martha and Penny Varney. The rest of the book was filled with entries. "Do you mind if I take this along?"

"Just so I get it back when you're finished." There was a hint of despair in Varney's tone, as though the book might eventually become a memento of the daughter he'd lost forever.

By the time they went back downstairs, Pearl Varney was waiting for them. She had set up a card table in her brother's study. On it were cups of hot milk and a plate of cookies.

"I made them myself," she said as if anything else were unthinkable.

"Aren't you going to join us?" Traveler asked her.

She looked to her brother for guidance. When none came, she shook her head and left the room.

"Please," Varney said, "help yourself."

Traveler sampled a cookie. It was filled with raisins and spiced with nutmeg and cinnamon. His stomach was immediately grateful.

He went through another cookie before asking, "Would you take your wife back if she came home?"

"That's none of your business, Traveler."

Traveler smiled. For the first time in their conversation, the Mr. had been dropped from his name. It gave him a perverse satisfaction to say, "Maybe I ought to speak with your sister."

"Does that mean you're going to help us?"

He thought about the white room upstairs filled with teddy bears that looked as if they'd never been hugged. "I'll do what I can."

Varney insisted on shaking hands again. As he did so he drew a deep breath. His chest expanded. A smile came to his face. He had the look of a man who has suddenly been relieved of a great burden. "You'll find Pearl in the kitchen." With that, he turned his back and began studying his *Book of Mormon*.

The kitchen was old-fashioned enough to have walls of tile, once white but now yellowed with age. The tiles on the floor were the same color, only much larger squares. Everything else had been updated, including a stove and refrigerator that gleamed like polished brass.

Pearl Varney, who had her back turned, was mopping bloody footprints from the floor. Traveler froze in midstep until he saw the pair of knee-high rubber boots off to one side, their soles and sides matted with bright red mud.

When he cleared his throat, she swung around, obviously startled. Her complexion was as white as snow. One hand went to her chest.

"I didn't mean to frighten you."

"Dear God, I thought you were a ghost."

6

Traveler thought he was seeing a ghost, too, as he left the house. Or perhaps it was his imagination that there had been movement in the aspen grove.

He stared into the blowing snow until his eyes watered. After a moment he shrugged, put his head down, and trudged toward the car. But as he pulled open the door, he glanced back one more time. The figure gliding through the trees, even blurred as it was by falling snow, was definitely not an apparition.

As a distraction, Traveler snapped his fingers like a man who'd forgotten something and slowly began plodding back toward the house. Halfway there, at a point where the walkway took him nearest the aspens, he veered suddenly and charged into the trees.

The ghost ran. From behind he looked like a three-hundred-pound lineman rushing some unseen quarterback.

Traveler's tackle knocked the man facedown in the snow. Air whooshed out of him. When Traveler rolled him over, the man's mouth was working furiously, spitting out snow while trying desperately to pull oxygen into his lungs.

The man wasn't really big. He was all clothes, bulky layers of them to protect against the cold.

Traveler straddled him, using his knees to pin the man's arms at his sides. Almost gently, Traveler wiped snow from his victim's face.

"I've seen you before," Traveler said, unable to attach a name for the moment.

By now the man had recovered enough strength to struggle. But he didn't have the mobility to free himself.

"Let me up," he said breathlessly.

"I remember now. You're Reuben Dixon."

Traveler eased back on his heels before slowly rising to his feet.

Immediately Dixon began feeling around in the snow. "I've lost my glasses."

"That's what you get for spying on people."

"Here they are, you bastard." Dixon clamped a glove between his teeth and pulled it off. His bare fingers trembled as he wiped snow from the lenses. Then he slipped on the glasses, blinked, and said, "I ought to sue you for assault."

Traveler bent over and helped the man to his feet. "I haven't assaulted you . . . yet."

Wide-eyed, Dixon backed away until he found himself pinned against an aspen. Snow tumbled onto his head from the overburdened spring leaves.

"You aren't going anywhere until I get some answers," Traveler said, moving in so close they were almost touching.

Dixon's head swung from side to side as if seeking a route of escape. He had a narrow skeletal face and eyes that were always on the move. His cheekbones jutted out sharply, adding to his death's-head appearance, while his bulky clothing made him look like a robot that was being operated from the inside by a much smaller man.

Traveler knew him to be a professional documents dealer who specialized in Mormon memorabilia. In the past he'd unearthed pioneer manuscripts purported to be signed by the likes of Joseph Smith and Brigham Young. Many of these contradicted present-day church policy. Such contentious documents brought a handsome price on the open market, despite those who claimed that Dixon was nothing but a forger out to make money off the church. Still others called him the anti-Christ. Nothing illegal had ever been proved against him.

Traveler grabbed a handful of clothing and shook Dixon until his head flopped back and forth. "I want answers from you," he said before releasing his grip.

Dixon's head continued to bob on its own.

"Why are you watching me?"

Dixon's head came to a sudden halt. He looked Traveler in the eye. "My clients, like yours, are entitled to privacy."

"What is that supposed to mean?"

"That I know a lot of important people. Their names might surprise you."

"Try telling that to the police when I have you arrested for trespassing."

The man suddenly looked smug. "Charges like that would be up to the Varneys. This is their property we're standing on."

Traveler thought that over. It was impossible to imagine a man like John Varney dealing with the likes of Reuben Dixon. Unless, of course, it was a matter of protecting the church.

"Who's to say I didn't lose my way in the storm?" Dixon went on. "I could have wandered in here by mistake."

Again, Traveler seized the man, this time with both hands, twisting the outer layer of material around Dixon's neck until he went up on tiptoe to avoid being choked.

"You don't have to prove how tough you are," Dixon panted. "Word about you is already out."

"It's all true," Traveler said, lifting Dixon off his feet and slamming him against the tree trunk so hard chunks of snow rained down on them from the quivering branches overhead.

The force of the impact caused Dixon's teeth to snap. "I bit my tongue," he yelped, spitting bright blood into the white snow.

Traveler pulled back for another try at dislodging the aspen.

Dixon's face puckered in anticipation. Then all at once his head sagged to one side and words began spilling out. "Okay. I came here to do a deal with Varney. We've worked together before."

"You'll have to be more explicit than that." Traveler again raised Dixon partially off his feet.

"Give me a chance," the man whined. "I've done a lot of favors for the church, goddammit."

Traveler allowed Dixon's feet to settle firmly on the ground. "And you're here to do another favor, is that it?"

"Exactly," Dixon said, missing Traveler's sarcasm. "You remember the Salamander letter?"

Traveler nodded.

"Well, what I've got now makes that look like"—his hands flapped to indicate a lack of words—"like child's play."

The Salamander letter was purportedly written by a contemporary of Joseph Smith in Palmyra, New York. In it, the church founder is said to have been a treasure hunter and a man who conversed with spirits that turned into salamanders. Such an image was a far cry from the present-day depiction of Smith receiving the golden tablets of Mormonism from the Angel Moroni.

"You can't sell anything out here hiding in the trees," Traveler said. "Or were you waiting for the ink to dry?"

"Don't blame me for being careful, not when I see a guy with your reputation drive up. One look at you and I told myself, 'Reuben, don't you make a move until you know just what the hell is going on around here.' So I decided to lay low, especially since I was holding a hot potato like this one. For all I know, Varney got wind of my find and brought you in to take it away from me, thereby saving the church a lot of money."

Traveler didn't know what to think. One thing was certain. He wanted nothing to do with church politics. Still, he was curious. He also figured there was a good possibility that Dixon was lying.

With a scowl Traveler drew back a fist and muttered, "Maybe it's time I added to my reputation. Unless, of course, you want to tell exactly what it is you're selling."

"Go ahead. Hit me. But nobody gets a look at this without paying first."

Traveler pulled his stomach punch. Even so, Dixon crumpled in the snow, curling into a ball and gasping for breath. "Bastard," he managed after a moment.

Traveler knelt beside him. "I don't like violence."

"Sure," Dixon croaked.

"Now, tell me how much you're asking."

Dixon grinned. "More than you can afford."

7

Traveler remembered the old police station on First South and State. It had been a landmark, three stories of red sandstone, granite steps and cornices, a kind of Victorian hand-me-down that had died beneath the wrecker's ball. Its concrete and brick replacement on Fourth Street and Third East possessed all the charm of a parking garage.

Lieutenant Anson Horne went with the building. He was solidly built, the same muscled width from shoulders to waist, with hostile blue eyes and unruly blond hair on the verge of turning gray.

He pinned a visitor's badge to Traveler's damp coat and said, "I was hoping I'd never hear from you." Without waiting for a response he led the way to a half-walled, six by six cubicle at one end of a forlorn squad room painted a dingy white. Smiling unhappily, he slid behind a desk that was too large for such cramped quarters, leaving Traveler to settle his bulk onto an undersize metal chair that was bolted to the floor.

"Not quite the luxury private eyes expect," Horne said, leaning back and hooking his thumbs behind bright red suspenders. The gesture exposed a chrome-plated .357 magnum.

When he saw Traveler eyeing the weapon he asked, "Are you carrying?"

Jesus, Traveler thought, spreading his coat. Was this the red-carpet treatment that Will Tanner had promised?

"For once," Horne said, "our metal detectors seem to be working. I understand you collect guns."

"World War Two rifles mostly."

"They aren't much good at close quarters."

"I have a permit to carry a gun, if that's what you're asking."

"I'm not asking anything. I was just wondering about you. Like how long you've been in town?" His tone said he didn't expect an answer. "Five months, isn't it? Maybe six. It usually takes nine months for a concealed weapons permit to go through. But then I'm forgetting about your friends, aren't I? It's not everyone who has a Willis Tanner to vouch for him. But what the hell. We in the police department love you anyway."

"Come on, Horne. A man's got to be able to protect himself in our business."

"But it never hurts to have important connections, does it? Take me, now." He snapped his suspenders. "Influence got me where I am today. That and fifteen years' hard work. What you see before you is a second-generation cop. Some say that makes me a dummy, because I should have known better. The plain fact is, my father told me to be a plumber. There at least, he said, you can recognize real shit when you see it. Around here you never know when you're going to land in something worse."

"I'm just an enlisted man, Horne. You're the lieutenant."

"Un-hunh," the cop said, forcing a smile. "Now tell me just what the fuck I can do for one of Utah's great football heroes?"

"That's ancient history."

"They still show you on highlight films."

"That's why I stopped watching television," Traveler said, hoping that Horne would drop the subject.

"If I remember correctly you got a full scholarship to USC, didn't you?" Horne winked to show there was no envy, but his eyes said otherwise.

"If it makes you any happier, I never graduated. I spent four years taking two years' worth of classes."

"That didn't stop you from signing a big bonus with the pros."

Here it comes, Traveler thought. People just wouldn't let the past die. They had to keep reminding him, though God knows why. His nightmares already took care of that.

But the cop surprised him. He didn't talk football. Instead, he stretched his suspenders almost to the breaking point and said, "Willis Tanner ought to have known better than to call in a private ticket on something like this."

Traveler shrugged. "Just what did my old pal Willis have to say?"

"To keep you informed about the dead guy." He snapped his suspenders. "Like letting you know he was humping the Varney broad before he left Arizona for Bountiful."

"I hope you can do better than that."

"You're not one of us."

"One of who?" Traveler was being deliberately obtuse.

"LDS, goddammit."

"Good Mormons don't swear."

Horne flushed. A vein stood out on his forehead. "My father warned me about you and your family. He had the misfortune to work with your father a long time ago."

My God, Traveler thought. Salt Lake may have grown big enough to look like a cosmopolitan city, but it was still a small town at heart.

"I've been asked to help you," Horne went on. "Well, asked isn't exactly the right word. So I'll do my duty."

"Is there anything I ought to know about the Bountiful killing?"

"Private detectives don't work murder cases."

"I'm not exactly thrilled by the situation, either."

Horne stared. "You know something, I don't think you are at that." He shrugged and began massaging his temple. "I gave a copy of the report to Tanner. What else do you want?"

"That was the prelim, filed by the first cops on the scene. I want to know what follow-ups have been made."

For a moment the cop looked as if he were about to object. Then he got on the phone and started making calls.

A few minutes later he hung up and said, "We've come up with a half-assed witness who says he saw a blond woman go into the dead man's house. He'd probably ID you in a wig."

"What kind of gun was used?"

"A forty-five. Your kind of gun, right out of World War Two."

Traveler smiled dutifully. "I ran into a man named Reuben Dixon on the way here. He was hiding in the trees outside the Varney place."

The policeman stiffened.

"He told me he was there to sell documents to Varney. Would you know anything about that?"

"A year ago that bastard was running a shoestring operation. Now he suddenly has money to burn. He has to be screwing it out of somebody, that's for sure. Probably the church."

Traveler hadn't expected that kind of candor, not from one of the chosen people. "What do you know about the Church of Zion Reborn?"

"Enough to want it burned to the ground." Horne chuckled nastily. "If they had a goddamned church."

Traveler stared at the cop. Horne wouldn't be the only one with that kind of attitude. In this town the police department would be full of officers who thought of themselves as modern-day Avenging Angels, spiritual descendants of Brigham Young's nineteenth-century vigilantes. The same kind who were responsible for the Mountain Meadow Massacre.

Traveler started to rise. Horne waved him back into the seat, then closed his eyes and vigorously rubbed his forehead. "A word of advice. I don't want you getting into trouble. My father said your old man was an expert at that. Like father, like son, eh?"

Traveler folded his arms and waited.

Horne went on. "I heard you put some guy in the hospital down south. The wrong guy, some say. Others say you just plain like to hurt people. It doesn't much matter who."

"No complaint was ever filed."

"Sure, because you paid the bills." He shrugged. "That's what I heard, anyway. I also hear the guy you flattened was one of many standing in line to bang your girl."

Traveler held himself perfectly still, saying nothing.

"From what I hear, your father was the same kind of hothead. Broke a few bones in his time, too." The cop smiled. "I figure you've decided to take up where your old man left off."

"My father is retired."

"I don't think there's enough work in this town for one private eye named Moroni Traveler," he said. "Let alone two."

8

Only a dozen steps from the police building Traveler felt lost in time. Snow was falling so heavily it was like a curtain shutting off past and future, leaving him with only a cold white present.

Shivering, he pulled the flimsy collar up around his ears and ran for the parking lot. Inside the car, he revved the engine hoping to encourage the heater. It blew enough but produced no heat, only a noxious smell. His damp clothes didn't help the atmosphere either.

That settled it. Despite the fact that he was aching to get his hands on Reuben Dixon again, Traveler decided to go home. Besides, Martha Varney had been missing for a long time now. With luck another few hours wouldn't make any difference. And with more luck the city's snowplows would have the streets cleared by morning.

Or so he thought until he started driving. Nighttime visibility, limited to a few yards when he started out, got worse as he drove toward the higher elevation of the avenues. Drifts were already more than a foot deep in places. Tree limbs, overloaded with snow trapped in their spring leaves, littered the streets.

On top of everything else, the tire chains were shaking what life was left right out of his Ford. By the time he parked in front of the house on First Avenue an hour later, he had the sensation that he'd driven across the state instead of the four miles from downtown.

The house, with adobe walls two feet thick, was a relic from pioneer times. At the moment it looked like an igloo with green shutters.

Traveler felt like a snowman by the time he made it to the front door. His father, Moroni Sr., who preferred to be called Martin, met him at the door. "Mad Bill called and warned me you'd be late."

Traveler stomped his feet, which was a mistake because that started them tingling with chilblains. "How did he know that?"

"He said you were involved in church business. Is that true?"

"Fix me a hot drink while I get undressed. Then we'll talk."

Traveler kicked off his shoes and realized that he couldn't feel his toes. To bring them back to life, he began rubbing his feet along the carpet as he made his way toward his bedroom, the same one he'd had as a child. It stood at the end of a long hall, past a wide spot with a southern window known as the sun porch.

His room, separated from the rest of the house like an afterthought, still contained his childhood furniture, early American replicas from the forties.

"I'm not a sentimental man," his father explained

when Traveler had returned six months ago. "It just seemed a waste to buy new things."

To which Traveler merely nodded. Anything more would have embarrassed both of them.

As usual the bedroom was cold, since hot air had such a long way to come from the basement furnace. Traveler quickly shed his clothes, leaving them on the linoleum where they fell. The flooring, simulated wood to go along with real knotty-pine walls, still contained the burn marks where he'd experimented with cigarettes as a youngster. He and his best friend at the time, Will Tanner, had gone through an entire pack in one day, with Will squinting over his shoulder after each puff expecting to see an angry Mormon God.

Naked, Traveler hurried into the shower, running hot water until the bathroom warmed with steam. Then he plunged under the spray, dancing in and out to keep from being boiled. When he'd warmed up enough to relax, he added cold water to the flow. Only then did he stand directly under the spray and soak.

Finally, he reached for the soap and began washing himself. By the time he got to his toes, feeling was beginning to return.

The musty shower smell, the cold concrete floor chilling his bare feet, his own anxieties, all served to trigger a flood of memory. He was a child again, hiding in that same shower, because it was the farthest he could get from his parents' room without actually leaving the house. Usually, with the bathroom door closed, the distance was enough to reduce their arguments to unintelligible sounds. But not this time.

Even now, with so much time elapsed, he could recall everything, how he pulled a blanket from his bed and dragged it into the shower, wrapping it around himself as he huddled in the corner, praying that shower spiders wouldn't drop down his neck.

Finally, in desperation he had covered his head but that only muffled the words. He could still understand what was being said.

I wish it wasn't true, but he's not my son. His father's voice.

I named him after you, from his mother.

A woman's kind of conscience money, no doubt.

You left me alone.

I went to war.

Soldiers, his mother laughed. *It's all right for them to screw everything in sight.*

I didn't.

Then I made up for both of us, didn't I?

The hot water ran out. Shivering again, Traveler stepped from the shower and rubbed himself warm.

When he walked into the living room a few minutes later, wearing flannel pajamas and a heavy terry-cloth robe, his father was already standing in front of the fireplace holding two cups of steaming coffee.

"You were a long time," he said.

"I was cold."

"I heard you talking to yourself."

Traveler didn't remember giving voice to his thoughts. "What did I say?"

With exaggerated nonchalance his father concentrated on his coffee. After a prolonged silence he said, "I read somewhere that environment is more important than heredity. Experts consider everything outside the egg cell as environment, you understand."

Traveler grunted. The coffee burned his tongue.

79

"Damn near anybody can make themselves a family," his father went on. "It's what happens after that counts."

Traveler did something he hadn't done in years. He hugged his father, squeezing until the old boy gasped, "Let me go, for Christ's sake."

The moment Traveler released him, Martin stepped back. "If I didn't know better I'd say you were still growing." He stood on tiptoe to make himself taller. "But they tell me it's us old people who are shrinking."

Traveler grinned. At times like this he knew that whatever he was, both good and bad, he owed to Martin. Likes and dislikes, even prejudices, all had been absorbed over the years. But there was more to his inheritance than that, practical things that Martin had taught him. How to cut a pocket from an old pair of trousers and use it as a money pounch pinned inside your waistband. Or how to disarm a man.

"We're very much alike," Traveler said. And yet so different, he thought. But heredity or not, I am your son.

Physically they were opposites. Martin was short, five feet six inches before age took its toll. Traveler was six three the last time he checked.

On a good day Martin weighed a hundred and forty pounds. Traveler tried to keep his weight at two hundred, though he'd played football nearer two forty. He'd gone as high as two fifty when he joined the Los Angeles Police Department after retiring from professional football. On the force he thought bulk would be on his side. Instead, his size had attracted every macho asshole who wanted to prove a point.

For a long time neither of them spoke. The silence was broken only when a log settled in the grate, causing sparks to shower against the fireplace screen like angry insects.

Absently his father brushed the seat of his pants. Then he ran his feet back and forth over the carpet in front of the hearth as if stamping out embers. "I never like to go to sleep until a fire's out," he said.

"I'll wait up with you," Traveler answered as he eased himself into a reclining chair that squeaked as it unfolded.

On the mantel behind Martin stood family photographs spanning forty years. They had been arranged chronologically from left to right. The oldest, a wedding picture of Martin and Kary, was enshrined in a silver frame. Next to it, overpowered by a heavy oak frame, was Martin as a young man. He was wearing his army uniform from World War II, a subject that had been taboo for years.

In fact, Traveler couldn't recall his father ever speaking about the war, though his mother had made a few choice comments on rare occasions. "Your father was a goddamned hero. That's hard for a woman to live with, I can tell you. It always made me feel guilty."

In the beginning Traveler hadn't understood what she had meant.

Next came photos in cardboard holders. In one of them a bald-headed man stood next to a 1941 Cadillac. His face was slightly out of focus. To this day Traveler didn't know the man's name, though he suspected it might be his biological father.

Whenever he'd asked about it, Martin had said,

"That's one thing you'll have to speak to your mother about."

But all she would say was, "The man's dead now. So what difference does it make?"

"Is he part of our family?"

A faraway look would come into her eyes.

"Why do you keep him on the mantel then?" Traveler had persisted quite logically.

His mother had gone to her grave without answering that question. One day, he promised himself, he'd take time out to investigate that face personally. The idea made him think about Penny Varney, who was conducting her own kind of search.

The photograph on the far right showed Traveler as a senior linebacker at USC. The picture of him playing for Los Angeles had been removed after the accident.

Martin slid one of the photos aside to make way for his empty coffee cup. "Did I tell you that Mad Bill called?"

"The moment I came in the door."

"Was he right? Are you working for the church?"

"For Willis Tanner, actually. But that amounts to the same thing."

"I knew that boy was going to cause trouble the moment his family moved in next door." Martin snatched up his cup, glaring into it as if someone had stolen his last swallow. "Even after he became a deacon he was a wild kid. Did I ever tell you what I caught him doing behind the house?"

"I was there, too, remember."

He snorted. "That's right." He waved his cup. "Let's have a refill."

"No more coffee. It keeps me awake."

"Exactly. Stick to brandy. It's better for you."

A cup in each hand, Martin disappeared into the kitchen. He returned almost immediately carrying glasses and a bottle. "You working for the church makes me want to get drunk."

"That's two of us."

"As good a toast as any." His father filled the glasses beyond discretion. "Here you are, my boy. I have a feeling you're going to need it."

Traveler warily accepted the glass.

"There's something else I have to tell you," his father said, downing his brandy and then coughing like a man who didn't really have to. "There was another call for you."

His tone of voice made Traveler ask, "Claire?"

Martin sighed. "She left a number."

That was something different. "Where is it?"

"On the pad by the phone."

Traveler started to get up, but his father waved him back into the recliner. "She said it would be good only until eight."

Martin checked his watch. "It's long past that now." He caught his son's reproving frown and added, "It was already too late by the time you got home."

"I'll give it a try anyway."

His father reached out to him then, touching him lightly on the arm. The gesture was both shy and restraining. "Son, she's got too many troubles of her own."

"Hindsight is a wonderful thing."

"I could have predicted the future for you when you first met her. But would you have listened?"

Traveler shrugged.

"Hell no. Nobody ever does. You know that." Martin took up his wedding picture like a man handling high explosives. "Everyone has to make his own mistakes. Thank God you didn't marry yours."

Traveler went to the phone, his father right behind him.

"You're not going after her, are you?"

"I hope not."

He dialed the number on the pad. A man answered, shouting over background noise that sounded like jukebox music at a bar.

"Is Claire Bennion there?"

"Shit, fella, somebody ought to beat some sense into you, keeping a nice lady like that waiting all this time."

"Tell her it's Moroni."

"There's a fucking angel on the phone," the man shouted before breaking into laughter. A chorus of bar voices joined his merrymaking.

When it finally subsided Claire came on the line to ask breathlessly, "Is that you, Moroni?" She sounded as if she, too, had been laughing.

"None other." He forced himself to sound light-hearted.

"Guess where I am?"

"A bar."

"You really are a detective."

"Detective angel," someone whooped in the background.

"I need you," she said.

"You know where my father lives."

"Oh, no. You have to find me. You know that."

"I've given up."

84

"You'd come looking if someone were paying you."

"No one is."

"I'd pay you with love."

"It's late. I'm tired."

"If you don't find me this time, it will be too late."

"It's already too late."

"You'll have to live with the consequences if you don't."

"What consequences, Claire?"

"You'd have to be a real angel to know that, Moroni."

9

Sleep turned out to be as elusive as Claire. Finally Traveler groaned in frustration, switched on the bedside light, and went to work on the address book that had belonged to both Varneys, mother and daughter, reading through it methodically, starting with the A's. Surprise came four letters later. In what appeared to be the more recent handwriting, there was a listing for R. Dixon. No address was given but there was a phone number.

Fueled by a sudden surge of adrenaline, he snatched up his watch from an early American chest of drawers that had once served as a landing strip for his model airplanes. For a moment he thought the second hand had stopped moving. Then he heard ticking and realized the time was correct, two o'clock in the morning, too late to do anything except go back to sleep. But the thought of Reuben Dixon, compounded by the coffee, or the brandy, or both, had him wide awake.

With a sigh of resignation, he went back to the address book. But after a couple of pages he realized it was no use. He knew himself too well. He was going to call R. Dixon no matter what the time.

Barefoot, he tiptoed down the hall past his father's bedroom, through the dining room, and into the alcove that held the phone. He let it ring for a long time without getting an answer. Three possibilities came immediately to mind: the man wasn't home, he was a heavy sleeper, or he was refusing to answer. Of course, there was always the chance that Traveler was calling an entirely different R. Dixon. But he didn't believe in coincidences like that.

Then it hit him. Use your head. Look it up in the phone book.

Sure enough, the number in the address book matched Mountain Bell's listing for Reuben Dixon. The address given was on Edgemont Avenue, only a few blocks north of the temple.

He woke his father to borrow the jeep, which had four-wheel drive and a new set of snow tires.

"I don't think this is a good idea," Martin said groggily. Then he saw the look in his son's eyes. "Do you want me to come with you?"

"I can take care of myself."

"Not when the church is involved," Martin said, slipping out of bed to grab hold of his pants which he'd abandoned over the back of a chair. He fished car keys from a front pocket and held them out. "Be careful."

The Edgemont address turned out to be one of those bleak three-story apartment buildings that had gone up in the thirties. Traveler had been inside enough of them to know they were all the same: four apartments on each floor. There would be a plaque, usually brass, next to the door with an imposing name, something like The Centurion or The Cambridge.

His knowledge came from a summer job his father had wangled for him delivering furniture. Invariably the buildings had one small elevator that wasn't to be used by the likes of workmen. As a result he'd hauled hide-a-beds, sofas, and even a piano up narrow service stairs on more than one occasion.

Traveler smiled with satisfaction at the brass plaque—The Villa. An overhead light protected by wire mesh cast just enough of a glow to illuminate the names on a row of brass mailboxes. There were listings for two Dixons: R. Dixon, Apt. 12, and V. Dixon, Apt. 3. If The Villa ran true to form, number twelve would be on the top floor.

The catch on the downstairs door was clogged with snow, so Traveler walked right in. He avoided the old-fashioned elevator because it was sure to make a racket, and followed a trail of slushy footprints up the carpeted stairs.

The slush ran out at the second floor. But wet footprints went all the way to the top.

As Traveler climbed, the building's odor intensified. By the time he reached the top floor the smell was strong enough to taste, like an old meal partially regurgitated.

Scuff marks on the carpet at the head of the stairs indicated that whoever left the tracks had stopped to wipe his shoes. After that, Traveler had no footprints to follow, though when he touched the carpet directly outside number twelve the nap felt slightly damp.

He rang the bell. In the still of the night it sounded loud enough to wake the dead.

After a moment he heard a crash, as if something had been knocked over. "Shit," a man muttered. Footsteps clopped. The door opened.

In a bathrobe Dixon looked a hundred pounds lighter than he had earlier in the evening. His feet were in galoshes instead of slippers. One look at Traveler and he said, "Shit," again, immediately adding, "do you know what time it is, for God's sake? It's the middle of the night." Dixon's breath smelled of whiskey. "What happened? Did John Varney send you here to scare the goodies out of me?"

Traveler smiled, hoping to keep the man talking. Without being asked, he stepped across the threshold and into a small, dimly lit hallway. Straight ahead stood a closed door, probably the bathroom. On his right was an open archway. He followed Dixon through it.

Obviously Dixon used his living room as an office. Along one wall was a cluster of tan metal filing cabinets, their top forming a counter of sorts on which folders were heaped. Next to the cabinets stood a rolltop desk from whose open mouth papers spilled like an unruly tongue. A brass goosenecked lamp curved out from the wall, its bright bulb throwing a pool of light on the disgorged papers.

Dixon turned abruptly, his hands up as if to fend off attack. "If you're here to hit me again, I'm going to start screaming bloody murder. My neighbors have orders to call the police if I call for help."

"I'll have whatever you're drinking," Traveler said, indicating a lone, two-drawer filing cabinet that was being used as a makeshift bar.

Smiling slyly, Dixon poured bourbon into two

glasses, added ice and a dash of diet 7-Up. "Let me see you drink it," he said, handing the glass to Traveler.

Traveler obliged, swallowing half the contents in a gulp.

"That's all right, then," Dixon said. "Varney wouldn't send a Jack Mormon to do his dirty work."

Traveler smiled. Originally Jack Mormon had referred to gentiles who befriended members of the church. More recently the term had become a designation for Mormons who'd strayed from Joe Smith's Word of Wisdom.

"Why are you here?" Dixon said.

Traveler saw no harm in telling the truth. "I thought you might be able to help me locate Martha Varney."

"So that's what you were doing at the house."

"Yes."

"Let me tell you something. I wouldn't raise a fuckin' finger to help John Varney. I went to him in good faith, gave him a fair price, and what did he do? Turned me down flat." Dixon added whiskey to his own drink, ignoring Traveler's half-empty glass. "Doesn't he realize what my document could do to that beloved church of his?"

Dixon peered intently at Traveler, blinking like a man having trouble focusing. After a moment his free hand made a circling motion to show he was waiting for some kind of answer.

Traveler said, "I imagine that means you're not a member of the church yourself."

"Damn right I am. How else would I get access to records for my research?"

"What if I told you it's not John Varney I'm working for?"

"I'd say you were smarter than you look, then. Varney's a loser, for Christ's sake. He should have paid me my money. It's not coming out of his pocket. No, indeed. The church is loaded. Ten percent tithe from the faithful. And what do I ask? Peanuts. Anyone with brains would pay through the nose to keep a murder quiet."

The moment the last words were out Dixon pounded himself on the forehead with the palm of his hand. "Reuben, you're a dummy. The man's looking for Martha Varney, not religion."

Traveler finished his drink and put the glass down. "You're going to have to tell me about the murder, one way or another."

"I told you before. That's my secret. It's money in the bank. If John Varney won't pay, someone else will."

Traveler grabbed the man's bathrobe so hard seams ripped under the arms.

"For Christ's sake, you're as bad as Varney. This has nothing to do with Martha. The murder I'm talking about is a hundred years old, more. Ancient history."

Traveler balled his fist under Dixon's nose. His only reaction was to sigh, as if resigning himself to take whatever punishment was coming.

"All right," Traveler said after a moment. "We'll stick to Martha Varney."

"You can go ahead and beat me up for that, too. I don't know anything. If I did, I would have told Penny a long time ago."

"How do you know her?"

"Like me, she's another of the faithful who's gone astray."

"Your number was in her book."

"Maybe it was my wife's number. She used to live here, too, you know."

"And now?"

He snorted. "She has her own phone downstairs. Unlisted so I won't call her in the middle of the night when I'm drinking."

10

Apartment number three was on the ground floor. It was nearly four o'clock in the morning when Traveler rang the bell, with Reuben Dixon hovering just behind him.

"That's no way to do it," the man said, his voice slurring. He punched the bell, holding it down until Traveler pried his finger away.

"It'll do her good," Dixon said. "Put a little adrenaline in her blood for once."

"I'd better take you back upstairs. I can talk to your wife another time."

From behind the door a woman's voice said, "Is that you, Reuben?"

"Who else, for Christ's sake?"

"Have you been drinking again?"

"You're damn right."

"I'm sorry, Mrs. Dixon," Traveler said. "I'll try to put him to bed."

The door opened, though with a night chain in place.

Even viewed through such a small opening she appeared to be an elegant woman, with that special kind of pale-skinned beauty some achieve about forty. In contrast to her ivory complexion, her black hair and dark eyes looked all the more intense.

Smile wrinkles around her eyes and lips refused to go away when she frowned at him. "Who are you and what are you doing with my husband?"

Traveler showed her a photostat of his license.

She squinted at it. "Are you the police?"

"I'm a private detective, Mrs. Dixon." Then he stretched the point to add, "I'm working for the church."

The moment her eyes widened, she had that vague look the nearsighted get when caught without their glasses. "I knew it, Reuben. I always said you'd go too far and get yourself into real trouble."

"It's not me who's got the trouble."

"Go to bed and let me talk to the man."

When he started to argue, Traveler took hold of his shoulder and squeezed.

"All right," Dixon said, his voice rising with pain. "Sleep with her if you want. But you'll freeze your balls off." With that, he careened down the hallway. A moment later they could hear him bumping his way upstairs.

"I'm sorry," she said.

"I'm the one who should apologize, Mrs. Dixon."

"What's this about?"

"I'm trying to find Martha Varney."

She sighed. "You'd better come in then. We don't want to wake up the neighbors."

Her apartment, a duplicate floor plan of her husband's, was furnished thoughtfully. A large Oriental rug of gold and deep blue went nearly wall-to-wall in the living room, while powder-blue drapes masked all the windows. The same powder-blue was picked up in an overstuffed sofa covered in corduroy. There were also two matching wing chairs done in rose velvet, a Victorian needlepoint love seat, and a reclining lounger facing the television set.

But it was a straight-backed rocker in one corner that attracted Mrs. Dixon. Once settled into it, she immediately folded her hands in her lap. But she didn't rock. Instead, she kept her feet planted firmly on the floor.

"That poor child," she said. Her face changed. Tension pulled the skin tight around her eyes, erasing the wrinkles. Without them she looked old and forlorn. "She's still grieving for her mother."

"You mean Penny?"

"The Varneys are my cousins. Thanks to them, a little church work used to come my husband's way when times were hard."

"And now?"

The wrinkles around her eyes came and went. "My husband bought this building. He owns others, too. It's no longer money with him. It's . . ."

Traveler waited, hoping she'd continue. When she didn't he said, "Are you saying Martha Varney was an in-law?"

"More than that. We were friends once. But I've never forgiven her for leaving Penny. That child's never been the same."

"I'm told she was fifteen at the time."

Mrs. Dixon studied him thoughtfully. "Penny is years behind her real age. Because of it, people take advantage of her. I hope you're not one of them, Mr. . . ."

"Moroni Traveler."

"You're not LDS, are you?"

"Does it show?"

"As far as I'm concerned it does. I knew Reuben wasn't one of us the moment I saw him. But did I walk away?" She answered her own question with a shake of her head. "He thought it was funny when Penny lost her faith. I think he may have encouraged her. For that, I can't forgive him. Who else could have put such ideas in the girl's head? She actually went to the prophet, to Elton Woolley, behind her father's back and asked for Martha's baptism for the dead. Do you know what that means?"

He nodded.

"The family once considered getting professional help for that child."

"A psychiatrist?"

"It never went that far, Mr. Traveler. We Mormons like to do our own healing."

She looked down at her own hands as if they had the power to cure.

"When did you last see Penny's mother?"

"A long time ago." She made a show of counting on her fingers. "Three years at least."

"I was told that she left John Varney five years ago."

"That sounds right." Her eyes narrowed as though concentrating on a distant memory. "Martha came back to Salt Lake about three years after she left. She wanted to see Penny, but John wouldn't allow a reconciliation, or so Martha said when she came to see me after he turned her away. She'd been drinking by then and smelled like a saloon. I couldn't help feeling sorry for her, though, especially when she told me that she'd gotten down on her knees and begged John to forgive her. He's a hard man. Of course, I'm not saying he wasn't justified. But he should have left Martha's judgment to God and thought about his daughter a little more."

Mrs. Dixon's head tilted to one side and then the other as if she were listening for echoes from the past. "Martha used to talk about living in big cities like New York and Los Angeles. I hope she did. I hope she didn't get stuck like me." Her eyes went wide, giving her a startled look as if she couldn't believe what she'd just heard herself say.

Traveler wanted to reach out to her. Instead, he asked, "Do you know why she left John Varney in the first place?"

"I knew Martha back in high school. Even then she was different from the rest of us. Of course, that was twenty years ago. Things have changed since then. Salt Lake has become much more cosmopolitan. In those days there weren't many black or brown skins in this town. Heavens. There weren't many Catholics either. Martha was one of the few gentiles I knew. Yet somehow she became part of our group. She even came to Mutual with me a few times, though we both knew she did it to meet boys. That's where my cousin John fell in love with her."

Mutual, Traveler recalled from his own youth, stood for Mutual Improvement Association. In the early days it had provided theological studies for young people, but was now in the business of furnishing them

97

with wholesome recreation, usually on Wednesday evenings. In Mormon country, where the word was "be fruitful and multiply," that often translated into premarital sex.

"John must have been attracted to her because they were such opposites," Mrs. Dixon went on. "Marrying a Catholic twenty years ago was like marrying the devil."

She shuddered. "Maybe it still is. Maybe I should have known better, too. But Reuben joined the church for me. At least, he said it was for me."

Traveler nodded to keep her talking.

"If Martha had stayed on, John probably wouldn't have risen so high in the church. Certainly not to the Council of Seventy. He's lucky to have escaped the taint of Rome."

As she spoke Traveler kept wondering how an attractive, apparently intelligent woman could live forty or so years and still be fighting the religious battles that he had abandoned right along with puberty.

"If you ask me, it was John who drove her away. But to this day I don't know why. There was a time when I would have gladly traded places with her."

"Her husband for yours?"

"I was thinking about Penny," she said quickly, her eyes looking away, her cheeks flushing. "I never had any children of my own."

"Why do you and your husband live in separate apartments?"

"That's none of your business. But I'll tell you anyway, just to spite him. Once he started to make money selling documents, he changed. He chased women, the kind who are attracted to wealth. I could forgive him the women, but not the girl, not what he's done to Penny."

"Your niece has your husband's telephone number in her address book," Traveler said. "He claims that it was you she usually called."

"I only wish that were true, Mr. Traveler. Then perhaps I'd be able to forgive him."

11

Traveler awoke after an hour's sleep. It was still very early. When he stepped to the bedroom window, the white world outside looked silent and free of sin.

His eyes stung from lack of sleep. Rubbing them brought no relief, only tears.

"Don't eat yellow snow," his father shouted from the hallway.

"Are those your words of wisdom for the day?" Traveler's speech slurred and his tongue felt like a salted slug.

"Joseph Smith had his Word of Wisdom," Martin said, entering the room. "So do I. Stay away from the church. It's a hell of a lot more dangerous than yellow snow."

With an exaggerated groan, Traveler went into the bathroom to brush his teeth.

His father trailed partway, poking his head around the door frame. "The last time I went to church I married your mother."

Traveler gargled.

"Speaking of women," his father went on, "Claire called again."

"I didn't hear the phone."

"I thought that's what woke you. It did me. But that's women for you, always picking the wrong time and place. So I told her you spent the night out. You should have heard her then. In my day women didn't use that kind of language."

"Anything else?"

"Only that she wanted to be saved." The old man winked. "Don't we all."

"What the hell would I do without you, Dad?"

His father rubbed a thumb and forefinger together as if trying to get hold of just the right word. "For one thing, you probably wouldn't be a detective. I seem to remember your mother wanted bigger things for you."

"She had plans for me, all right."

Martin grimaced. "Big plans for a big man, she always said. That was one of the ways she took delight in pointing out the differences in our size."

Without thinking about it, Traveler found himself breathing shallowly, wondering if this would be the time when his father finally brought the question of paternity out into the open.

"Like father, like son, I used to tell her. God, it drove her crazy."

Traveler laughed out loud. It cleared his head; it reminded him just how lucky he was to have Martin as a father, genes or no genes.

Yet he could still hear his mother's answer to something like that. "Don't listen to your father," she'd say, the words *your father* pronounced reluctantly, as if somehow tainted. "Listen to me and you'll make something out of yourself. A big man has an edge in this life. People look up to him. Remember that and one day you'll thank me for steering you in the right direction.''

Whenever Traveler tried to argue she'd only talk louder. ''Add a profession to your size and you'll be something your father never was. *Important*. Why, if you were a doctor, or even a lawyer, there would be no stopping you.''

Traveler had once asked Martin what he thought of such grandiose plans. His father had stood on tiptoe measuring himself against a mark he pretended to have inked on his son's chest and said, ''What counts in life is being yourself. If there's a doctor inside there, he'll come out.''

''And if it's a lawyer?''

''Then God help us all.''

Traveler smiled at the memory and began lathering his face with shaving cream.

''Would you be open to an old man's advice?'' his father asked.

''Let's hear it.''

''There's a fire going in the living room. The refrigerator's full of food. I've got a fresh bottle of brandy. Why not take it easy and wait for the weather to break?''

''I don't remember you sitting back and putting your feet up when you were on a case.''

''Don't quote me my own habits.''

''That's what I thought,'' Traveler said, scraping at his whiskers.

''Normally I wouldn't say a thing.'' Martin's head shook. ''But how the hell can you work for a bunch of people who actually think they can turn themselves into gods through good deeds?''

" 'As man is,' " Traveler recited, " 'God once was; as God is, man may become.' " Or so the church believed. His father would have translated that as *keep your nose clean and one day you'll die, go to heaven, and be given a nice little planet of your own to play God with.*

"Aw, to hell with trying to talk some common sense into you," Martin said. "I'll go cook breakfast. You'll need a good meal to keep warm."

Ten minutes later Martin had bacon and eggs and sourdough toast on the table. They ate listening to the radio. The news was the same as usual, bad. But the weather forecast sounded hopeful.

When they were finished, his father made a face and pushed his chair back from the table. "The trouble with cooking is that food never tastes good when you prepare it for yourself. Let somebody else do the work and you can't stop shoveling it in."

With that, he poured them both a second cup of coffee. As soon as he sipped it he said, "This tastes like hell, too, but at least it's hot."

Traveler smacked his lips as was expected of him. His father shook his head in disgust. But Traveler knew he was pleased by the compliment just the same.

"Come on," the old man said gruffly, "let's take a look at the weather for ourselves."

He led the way out onto the porch, which ran across the entire front of the house, supported by wooden posts that got eaten by termites once a year.

Foot-long icicles hung from the roof with no sign of melting. Traveler blew out breath that billowed like cigarette smoke.

His father waded out into the snow and stared up at

the sky. When Traveler joined him, the old man pointed to a patch of blue directly overhead. "My father used to say that if there's enough blue in the sky to make a pair of breeches, that means an end to the storm."

"I thought you told me that applied only to rain."

"You remember that, do you?"

"I remember just about everything you've told me over the years." Traveler hugged his father around the shoulders.

"Let go," Martin complained. "I'm an old man, remember?"

"I don't feel so young myself at the moment. But what the hell. As long as the Jeep can move, I've got to keep looking for answers."

"I'll be here when you get back." Martin fought off a smile. "Where can I go without my car?"

"You told me yourself that it was a day for napping in front of a fire."

"There you go again, quoting me."

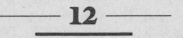

12

The money in Federal Heights rated special treatment when it came to snow removal. Even so, the roads were treacherous. Traveler passed only one other vehicle on his way to the Varney house, and it, too, had four-wheel drive.

When he got out of the car, the sun appeared briefly, casting black shadows against the snow. The momentary brightness left him seeing dark spots in front of his eyes as he approached the bleak brick house.

Pearl Varney answered the door, still playing her housekeeper role. She was dressed in black, like a widow.

"Yes?" she said as though she'd never seen Traveler before in her life.

He reminded her who he was.

"I wasn't told that you had an appointment." She positioned herself in the middle of the doorway to block his entrance.

"I came here looking for the truth," he said, conscious of sounding pretentious.

She glanced around as if it might be hiding behind

her. "Why don't you come back later. Better yet, telephone sometime this afternoon."

"All you have to do, Miss Varney, is tell me about the Dixons, and why you didn't let on about your relationship with them yesterday."

"I don't remember you asking. But all right. I admit it. I'm Virginia's cousin. But there's no blood between the Varneys and Reuben Dixon. He married into this family against our wishes."

"Then what was he doing here yesterday?"

She stared Traveler in the face, her eyes gradually narrowing. "He came to see my brother."

"You mean his cousin by marriage."

"If that's what you'd prefer."

"I'd better talk to your brother."

Pearl Varney hugged herself, gooseflesh showing where the dress failed to cover her neck. "He's not here."

"Where can I find him?"

"The president of the church called a meeting this morning. I doubt if you'd be welcome there."

"I'll tell you what. You give your brother a message for me. Tell him that I'll be sending the money back to Willis Tanner."

Panic showed in her face. "What do you mean?"

"I can't do my job if you and your brother hold back critical information. To my mind, your family's relationship with Reuben Dixon comes under that heading."

"My brother hired you to look after Penny's interests, not Reuben's."

"When I talked to Mr. Dixon, he sounded quite close to his niece."

"He's not the kind of man I would allow anywhere near Penny."

"And Martha?"

"Please," the woman said, a smile doing battle with her perpetual frown. When the frown won she reached out to him, taking hold of his arm and attempting to pull him inside. He resisted. "Right now Penny is all that counts, Mr. Traveler. I apologize if we've misled you."

He allowed himself to be tugged across the threshold. She let go of him only to close the door. After that, she led the way into the kitchen, where she quickly turned up the gas flame under a teapot that was already filled with water.

"Now," she said, "just what is it you want to know?"

"To start with, the details of Reuben Dixon's visit here yesterday."

The pot whistled. She turned away to spoon Postum into a pair of mugs, immediately adding boiling water, artificial sweetener, and milk. Caffeine-free Mormon coffee.

She handed him one of the cups before taking a tentative sip for herself.

"That's better." She wrapped hands around the hot porcelain. "Mr. Traveler, what good would come of finding Martha Varney after all these years? It would only cause Penny more heartache to see what kind of woman her mother has become."

"And what kind is that?"

"She's committed adultery. She admitted so in her own letters."

"Let's get back to Dixon."

With a quick shake of her head Pearl Varney pulled a heavily scented handkerchief from one sleeve and held it to her nose, taking several deep breaths. "I realize now that my brother should never have dealt with him. But when he married Virginia, what could we do?"

He caught the heavy fragrance of roses and tried to mask it with the taste of Postum, but that was just as bad. "What was Dixon selling yesterday?"

As if to give herself time to think, she sipped her drink, eyeing him coyly over the rim of her mug. Then she licked her lips, either policing up the Postum or trying to look provocative, he didn't know which.

"Are you married?" she asked, waving her handkerchief and scent in his direction.

He breathed through his mouth. "Dixon claims he came here with information about a murder."

She stiffened. "You mean that man in Bountiful?"

"A pioneer killing, he told me, back more than a hundred years."

She sighed, looking relieved. "That again. Reuben won't give up, I'll say that for him."

"I need more explanation than that."

"I'm not privy to all my brother's business dealings, Mr. Traveler."

He walked his Postum over to the sink. For a moment he thought about pouring it down the drain. Instead, he left it among dirty breakfast dishes. He couldn't think of any more questions. Besides, Pearl Varney wasn't answering them anyway.

He was about to say good-bye when John Varney stepped into the kitchen. The smile he'd been wearing dissolved into something approaching anger. "What are you doing here?" he demanded. "Why aren't you looking out for my daughter?"

"That's easy. Reuben Dixon sent me here to talk to you about a murder confession he tried to sell."

"Are you working with him?"

Traveler smiled. "You look guilty of something."

Varney clenched his jaw until his cheeks trembled with the effort. His hands fluttered as if trying to wave away unruly thoughts. "That's confidential church business."

"Now, John," his sister soothed, "don't get excited. It won't do your blood pressure any good."

Her comment set him off even more. "It's your fault, dammit. The moment Virginia married that man we should have cut them both off. But, oh no, you wouldn't hear of it. It was your idea to help them buy that apartment building of theirs."

He seemed to notice his restless hands and thrust them into his trouser pockets. "It's even on the wrong side of the tracks."

Jesus, Traveler thought, he hadn't heard that expression in years. But then, Mormon country was in its own special kind of time warp.

"Ginny is our cousin. We had to do the Christian thing by her," Pearl said, looking at Traveler as if speaking for his benefit. "The Varneys all come from the same small town in southern Utah, a place called Hurricane. Over the years we've stuck together. That's the way it should be."

Traveler stared suspiciously at her. "What about Martha Varney? Where did she come from?"

John Varney spoke up. "Nearby. Just over the border in Arizona."

Which, Traveler remembered, just happened to be near the headquarters of the Church of Zion Reborn.

"Do you have any relatives in that area now? Anyone Martha might contact?"

"Only those we buried there," Pearl Varney answered.

"Part of Hurricane just sort of dried up and blew away," her brother added. "Of course, in the early days when Brigham Young first colonized that portion of the state it was different. Southern Utah, even part of Arizona, was to be the new Dixie, a land of cotton to help subsidize the church." He sounded as though he would have preferred living back then. "But the climate was wrong. The crops didn't pay."

"Did Martha ever show any interest in family history?"

"No. Reuben's the one who makes money out of things like that."

"Why didn't you tell me about your connection with him yesterday?"

"He has nothing to do with my daughter."

"I hope you're right."

"Willis Tanner told me you were the best," Varney said, but his head shook as if denying the idea.

"Don't believe everything Will tells you," Traveler said. "I don't."

13

A bigger-than-life Jake Ruland, credit dentist, stood out front of his downtown office on Main Street, just up from the old Walker Bank Building. Technically, the eight-foot poster was in violation of city ordinances designed to keep sidewalks free of obstacles. But the blowup was Dr. Jake's trademark; it stood outside every one of his branch offices to indicate the place was open for business, no appointment necessary, dentures in a day.

Traveler's tongue probed his molars as he opened the door and stepped inside. Penny Varney's filling-free smile was the first thing he saw. It made him want to press his lips together until Dr. Jake could clean away the tartar.

"God loves a smile," she spieled before recognizing him. Her eyes widened. "Mr. Traveler, have you found my mother already?"

"Sorry. I have some leads. But I'd like to talk about them before I go any further."

He looked around the office. The waiting room was full. Most of the patients were older women.

"Maybe you could take a coffee break?" he suggested.

She rolled her eyes and whispered, "Doctor doesn't believe in coffee. It's not only a sin but stains the teeth."

"I could come back at lunchtime."

She pushed back from her uncluttered metal desk. Today she was dressed for winter, with a heavy blue sweater, a matching calf-length wool skirt, and white leather boots high enough to hide all signs of flesh.

"I'll get someone to sit in for me." She disappeared through a door marked "private."

While waiting, his tongue found a tender spot of gum behind one of his incisors. He was still worrying it when Penny returned. Dr. Ruland himself accompanied her. His appearance brought all the patients to their feet, a mark of respect or apprehension, Traveler couldn't tell which.

The dentist ignored his constituency to home in on Traveler. They shook hands. The man's grip would make yanking teeth child's play.

"Well?" Dr. Ruland said. When Traveler failed to respond the man added, "Everybody expects me to be as tall as my poster outside."

He was big enough, nearly Traveler's height, and just as impressive as his cardboard advertisement: an athletic-looking man in his late forties; black hair, no gray; a black, carefully trimmed beard; and dark flashing eyes. He belonged in *Wuthering Heights*, not a dental office.

"She's my lucky Penny," he said, smiling at his receptionist. His teeth, surrounded as they were by such an intensely black beard, seemed white enough to glow in the dark. "I wouldn't want anyone taking her away from me."

As he spoke, Penny retrieved a mock-fur coat from a coat rack behind her desk.

"I'd just like to borrow her for a few minutes," Traveler said.

Ruland snapped his teeth. Traveler found himself hoping they were capped.

"And so you shall," Ruland said, "even if I have to sit here at her desk myself."

Penny flushed. "It's not that important, Dr. Jake."

"That's right," Traveler picked up. "I can come back later, Dr. Ruland."

"Call me Dr. Jake. Everybody does. I insist on it."

Just then another girl came through the door marked private. Without waiting to be told, she took a seat behind Penny's desk.

"There you go," Dr. Jake said to Penny. "Take your time. You might as well make it a long lunch."

"But, Dr. Jake," Penny began.

"I insist." He slipped a hand against the small of her back, caressing while at the same time easing her toward the door. At the threshold he paused to help her on with her coat. He took the opportunity to lean close and whisper something in her ear. The look on his face was not that of an employer, but of a lover. Her look matched his.

God almighty, Traveler thought, what the hell did she see in a man more than twice her age? Power? Money? Her family already had those. She had to be another victim of Mormon country, where underground polygamy kept old farts supplied with young flesh.

Without warning a small man appeared next to the dentist. Traveler had the feeling that he'd been hiding behind Ruland all the time.

"Meet Brother Lehi," Ruland said, "my first acolyte."

Lehi didn't offer to shake hands but stood off to one side. Acolyte probably translated as bodyguard, though his size was hardly intimidating. Traveler remembered reading somewhere that men less than four feet eleven inches were considered abnormal. Below that were dwarfs and midgets. Lehi appeared to be slightly taller.

"He is a man possessed by God," Ruland said. "You can see that in his eyes."

What Dr. Jake interpreted as fervor Traveler saw as something verging on madness.

"People used to make fun of me," Lehi said.

Traveler, unsure of what response was expected, merely nodded. Penny's expression was somewhere between embarrassment and fascination.

"Leprechaun Lehi, they used to call me. Tom Thumb. Bug." His eyes, his body language, defied Traveler, anyone, to make such a remark now.

The dentist dropped a hand on his acolyte's shoulder and smiled benevolently.

"Men my size," Lehi said, staring at Penny, "are good with women." Dr. Jake chuckled and eased Penny out the door with a proprietary pat on the fanny.

Lamb's was the nearest restaurant. Since it was still snowing, that's where they went. As soon as they were seated Traveler said, "You didn't tell me about Dr. Jake."

"I gave you one of his cards."

"You know what I mean. That you're involved with him."

Penny shrugged. "That doesn't have anything to do with my mother."

"It affects your family, though."

Before he could press her further, a waitress arrived. Traveler ordered a prime rib sandwich the likes of which Lamb's had been serving since his childhood, while Penny settled for hot chocolate and an English muffin. Chocolate was also on the Mormon hit list, since it contained caffeine.

As soon as they were alone again he said, "Does your father know about Dr. Jake?"

"My father is too busy with his church to know anything else."

"He might surprise you."

"Has he bought you off, is that it? Are you here to tell me that you won't look for my mother?"

"Your father is worried about you, Penny."

She shook her head. "He knows how to get in touch with me."

"All right. It's none of my business. Now, if you want me to keep looking, Arizona seems to be the next logical place. In this kind of weather that means a full day each way, and maybe another there. Three days. With expenses that can run into a lot of money."

"Do you think you'll find her?"

"I can't make any guarantees. That's why I'm here."

"You find my mother and I'll pay you something every month if I have to, even if that means moving back home to save on rent."

14

The headquarters of the Mormon Church rises twenty-eight stories on South Temple, the tallest building in the state. It stands adjacent to the Hotel Utah on one side and Brigham Young's Lion House on the other. Security, though designed to look benign, rivals any police agency in the country. Traveler's two-man escort had the shining faces of believers who wanted nothing better than to smite a sinner.

From Will Tanner's office window the temple below looked foreshortened, less impressive than when viewed from ground level. The Angel Moroni and his trumpet flickered in and out of sight, depending on snowy wind gusts.

Tanner looked up from his computer terminal. "When the wind's just right, I can hear Moroni sounding his trumpet."

He'd spoken with that smiling squint of his, so that Traveler could read the statement as a joke if he wanted to. But Traveler knew better. Tanner was a man who'd heard the call of God all right. Whether it sounded like a trumpet or not made no difference.

He went back to staring at his computer screen. "John Varney called just before you got here, Mo. He said you've been asking some embarrassing questions."

"You can have your money back anytime you want."

Tanner held up his hands but continued to stare straight ahead. "What money?"

"That's right. The church isn't involved. You've never seen me before." Traveler settled into a chair in front of his friend's utilitarian desk.

"John Varney is an important man, Mo. I wouldn't want him for an enemy."

"You know me better than to make threats."

Again Tanner's hands went up in protest. This time he looked Traveler in the face when he spoke. "A little advice between friends is all I'm offering."

"What I'm after is information. Feed Dr. Jake Ruland into that machine of yours and see what happens."

"Are we talking church business or what?"

"You just told me the church has never heard of me."

Tanner sighed.

Traveler said, "Penny Varney is involved with the man."

"How?"

"At the very least she's his receptionist."

"And at the most?"

Traveler gestured at the terminal, which he knew was connected to a massive mainframe computer buried somewhere in the bowels of the building. No doubt every one of the faithful, plus the millions who'd been

117

raised to glory through baptism for the dead, were listed there. "Punch him in, Willis. I have a gut feeling that he's one of your black bishops."

Black bishop being Mormon-speak for highly placed saints who persist in following Joe Smith's word on polygamy, while the church hierarchy turns a blind eye.

"I happen to know he's a bishop in good standing."

"I see. I'm surprised you know all your bishops by name."

Instead of answering Tanner leaned toward his terminal, placed his fingers carefully on the keyboard, and typed in the name. After a moment he swiveled the screen so Traveler could read it from where he was sitting. Routine data appeared: name, date of birth (Ruland was forty-nine), place of birth (Lydel Springs, Arizona), record of tithing, and ward number and location.

"Anything else," Tanner said, "is confidential and requires a special access code."

"Is that how the black bishops are listed?"

"There's no such thing."

"I wish you could see that squint of yours. You never could lie well."

"Jake Ruland is a member of the church. That's the truth."

"How many wives does he have?"

Tanner swung the terminal screen back to its original position and hit more keys. "He's a widower."

"Then you don't care if Penny Varney becomes involved with him?"

"Why don't we put in your name, Moroni, and see

what we come up with?'' Without waiting for an answer he began typing.

Traveler left his chair to peer over his friend's shoulder. The green phosphorescent readout said, TRAVELER, Moroni: lost soul.

15

The sun broke through the overcast just as Traveler stepped from the LDS office building. The sudden light was blinding. He hadn't walked more than half a block before the snow underfoot started turning to ice. The sunshine was a lie, bringing cold instead of warmth. It also triggered a frenzy of drivers tired of being cooped up by the falling snow.

Traveler was just plain tired by the time he pulled into the driveway at home. For a moment he sat in the car unwilling to move, wondering if Martha Varney was anything like Claire. Perhaps neither one of them really wanted to be found. Maybe this search would be so much wasted effort.

Martin was asleep on the sofa, an empty glass on the TV set nearby. Flickering light from the tube cast shadows on his father's face, making his sleep look anything but peaceful. With the sound turned down, the soap opera characters on the screen had a dream-like quality about them, as if they were a projection of Martin's thoughts.

Traveler tiptoed all the way down the hill to the so-called sun room where guns were kept in a locked cabinet that had once been part of a built-in dressing table. He chose an old army-issue .45 and was loading an extra clip when his father came up behind him.

"What are you hunting, rhinoceros?"

"Polygamists."

"They're thicker skinned yet."

Traveler paused, loose ammunition in hand, waiting for the lecture that was to come. Martin, though the possessor of a fine arms collection inherited from his own father, did not believe in guns. He never carried one and, in fact, had turned down cases where weapons might be necessary. He'd had his fill of them in the war, a returning hero who had no use for soldiers.

"Jesus Christ," he said. "Polygamists and the church. You're asking for trouble."

"I'm going to a place called Lydel Springs," Traveler said. "It's just over the Arizona border."

"In that case I think there are some things we ought to talk about first."

"I want to be there before dark."

"At a time like this we don't want to leave anything unsaid between us."

"Don't go maudlin on me, Dad."

"We ought to clear the air about your mother and me."

For years Traveler had been waiting for just such an opportunity. But now was not the time to get distracted. "If all goes well I'll be back late tomorrow."

"You know best," Martin said in a tone that denied any such thing.

Traveler grunted noncommittally before struggling into a shoulder holster. When he slid the .45 into place, it seemed to increase in weight, making him lopsided. He hoped it wouldn't show beneath his heavy fleece-lined shearling coat.

He turned to his father, who was eyeing the pistol as if it disgusted and fascinated him at the same time. "I'd like to have my calls forwarded here while I'm gone."

"It will give a retired old man something to do, is that it?"

"If you don't want to be bothered, I can let my answering service handle it."

"I was always my own answering service. The personal touch, that was my motto."

There was no winning, Traveler thought. But he kept the notion to himself. Instead, he went to the phone and called his service, instructing the woman on duty to forward all inquiries to his father.

She carefully read back his directions before adding, "We have a call for you from someone named Bill. He left a number."

Traveler recognized the number; it belonged to the pay phone in the lobby of the Chester Building.

"He said it would be good through the cold spell," the woman added.

He thanked her, hung up, then dialed again immediately.

Charlie Redwine answered by saying, "How."

"This is Traveler. I got a message to call Bill."

Breaking precedent, Charlie abandoned his one-word vocabulary to report, "Bill's out right now having a new sandwich board made."

"Why did he call me?"

"It's important."

"I'm on my way to Arizona."

"I'll tell him."

"Shit," Traveler grumbled. This kind of weather raised hell with people like Charlie and Bill. The least he could do was make certain that they had eating money, though Barney Chester would probably be thinking the same thing. But Traveler wasn't about to take chances with friends. "Tell Bill I'll be there in a few minutes."

A half an hour later he found Mad Bill sitting cross-legged on the lobby's marble floor, a new sandwich board balanced across his lap. The placard read: THE GREAT FLOOD IS AT HAND.

"I don't get it," Traveler said.

"It's all clear to me now. The lake's rising. A second Noah is needed." Bill stabbed himself in the chest with his thumb. "I'm starting a campaign to raise funds for an ark."

"How much have you got so far?"

"Charlie has gone down to the Era Antiques to begin our crusade."

"I think I can manage a donation," Traveler said.

"You're a friend," Bill objected.

"What difference does that make?"

"I might not be able to deliver a real ark."

"What I had in mind was something to tide you and Charlie through the next couple of days until this weather breaks. Coffee money."

"No." Bill shook his head emphatically. "Charlie and I are fine. We're in God's hands."

Traveler, anticipating such reluctance, had taken a twenty from his wallet before entering the building. He'd folded the bill to hide its denomination.

But the sandwich prophet wasn't fooled. "We don't need this much for coffee."

"You never know what might come up."

Reluctantly Bill tucked the money into his jeans. "Charlie tells me you're taking a trip to Arizona."

Traveler nodded that he was. "The Church of Zion Reborn."

Concern pinched Bill's face. "Like I told you before, don't go messing around with those people. They deal in blood. One of them was killed in Bountiful yesterday."

"I'm after a missing person, Bill. A young girl's mother."

"Say no more. I know that look of yours. I won't waste breath arguing. But I can give you my blessing." Bill stood up, shedding his sandwich board, to make the sign of the cross. Traveler must have looked skeptical because Bill added, "It couldn't hurt, you know. A little faith."

"I've got to get going. Was there something else you wanted?"

Bill's head shook solemnly. "It's my duty to tell you." He stared up at the ceiling where Brigham Young was turning blacker by the day. "Claire came by here to see you."

"In person?"

"Yep," Bill said, still eyeing the competition overhead. "Hours ago."

What the hell was she up to? Traveler wondered. Always before she'd made contact on the telephone. "Did she say what she wanted?"

"I offered her my love as always. But it wasn't enough."

"If she comes back, hold on to her for me."

"You're talking about the woman I love. For her I'd give up all this." He gestured dramatically, his pointing finger finally zeroing in on the sandwich board. "Besides which, Barney has been giving me and Charlie dirty looks all day. I think he's trying to rent those empty offices of his. Our hanging around the lobby doesn't help. So me and Charlie figure we'd better disappear for a while."

"Here." Traveler reached into his pants pocket. "You can have the keys to my office."

16

Traveler felt himself begin to relax as he approached the town of St. George, in the heart of Utah's Dixie. The snow and icy roads were behind him. The weather was clear, the temperature warm enough to drive with the window rolled down.

Brigham Young had ordered the southern part of his state settled in 1861 to expand his empire, while at the same time securing his borders. His idea was to raise cotton in a region of mild winters. But southern Utah is a hard, unforgiving land, more beautiful than fertile.

Bright red cliffs, with local names like The Throne of Blood and The Devil's Hump, came into view. Here, even the soil was red. Legend had it that God gave his blood to the land but nothing else.

Since Traveler's last visit, St. George had grown. With expansion its character had disappeared. Instead of a charming relic from Utah's past, it now looked like just another suburban shopping center.

He passed up the usual fast-food franchises to dine at a place called The Dixie Queen, a ramshackle diner far enough off the main drag to have escaped progress. It was a single story of stucco complete with tin roof and old-fashioned venetian blinds in the windows, along with a neon sign that was having a hard time blinking out Coors.

The café reminded him of his childhood. So did the food, if the chalkmarked blackboard hanging behind the counter was to be believed. The vegetable of the day was fried turnips, something Traveler's mother had served him more times than he cared to remember. The special was a hot beef sandwich.

The counter, topped by red Formica simulating a kind of marble that had never existed, ran the length of the diner. What tables there were, unused and unset, looked as if they'd been rescued from the dump.

About a dozen customers filled every stool except the one right next to the cash register. The patrons, regulars by the looks of them, were all senior citizens. When they died so would The Dixie Queen.

As Traveler slid onto the vacant seat, the old man behind the register nodded as if such a greeting were part of a lifelong ritual.

"What do you recommend?" Traveler asked him.

He scratched his head as if considering a weighty question. "You can't beat the hot beef sandwich. This late that's all there is unless you want a hamburger."

"The hot beef it is, then."

"I don't take orders, only money."

Just then the waitress came through the kitchen door, fanning cigarette smoke away from her face. By the time she reached Traveler she smelled of peppermint.

The sandwich, when it came, consisted of thin strips of overdone meat laid out precisely on a slice of white bread. A scoop of mashed potatoes sat on one side of the plate, fried turnips on the other. Everything was smothered in a dark gravy.

Traveler gingerly tasted the beef. It reminded him of Woolworth lunches his mother had forced on him as a boy.

"Dessert goes with that," the waitress said. "We've got rice pudding. It's homemade."

Instead of pudding, he asked her for directions to the town of Hurricane, where the Varneys had been born.

"You've come too far," she said loud enough so that everyone in the place could hear too. "You should have cut off the interstate about ten miles back, where you pick up highway fifty-nine."

"I thought I'd better find a good place to eat first."

"You're right there, mister. Once you hit fifty-nine there's nothing at all. And I mean nothin'."

"And in Hurricane?"

"I've never tried to eat there myself." She looked down the row of customers. Several shook their heads as if agreeing with her assessment.

"My map isn't too clear. Do I hit Lydel Springs if I keep on fifty-nine?"

"Better you than me, mister."

When she didn't explain further, he said, "Why do you say that?"

"There have been a lot of killings in that area over the years. Some blame it on polygamists."

"You don't?"

"Strange things have been happening in this damn desert ever since the pioneers arrived." She wiped her hands on a gravy-stained apron that was cinched around her thick waist. "If you ask me, there're forces at work there that aren't human."

Such myths were rife in Utah, many of them fostered by the church in the early days to keep strangers out. If fear of the unknown didn't work, there was always the likes of Porter Rockwell, Brigham Young's avenging angel, to carry out the prophet's wishes. Or the secret society variously called the Brothers of Gideon, the Daughters of Zion, the Sons of Dan, or simply the Danites. Under whatever name, they murdered Indians and critics alike, anyone who threatened the Mormon empire.

"Come on, Ella," said the man behind the cash register. "Don't go spreading old wives' tales. Nobody who lives around here believes that stuff anymore."

"Maybe not. But I don't see any of you going out into that desert at night, either."

She stopped talking long enough to stare Traveler in the face. "Take my advice, mister. Stay here in town tonight and get a fresh start in the morning when it's light. When you can see what you're up against."

The old boy behind the register cleared his throat and asked, "Do you have business in Hurricane?"

By now everyone in the place had stopped eating and swung around on their stools to listen openly to the conversation.

"I'm trying to find someone who used to live there."

"Ella's right, then." He clicked his dentures. "Folks in Hurricane don't take to strangers much. Not in the dark anyway. Not that I blame 'em."

Traveler nodded. The man made sense. He couldn't

go knocking on doors in the dark. Besides, he needed sleep.

"I saw a lot of no vacancy signs coming into town," he said.

"That's because of the storm up north. It always backs up traffic," the old man replied. "Snow this late in the year is a real windfall for the motel owners."

"Any suggestions?"

The old man had a calling card ready. "It's the Dewdrop Inn down by the river where the old highway used to be. Nobody goes there now, so there's always plenty of room."

17

Hurricane looked like a typical small Utah town, clustered along State Highway 59. As Traveler parked in the center of the business district, the barren landscape beyond the city limits remained clearly visible. All vegetation in sight—trees, lawns, flowers—was the result of irrigation. It was a town under siege from the surrounding desert. But the townspeople he spoke with didn't seem affected by it. Despite the dire warnings of the night before, they were friendly and open, though no one remembered the Varneys, or Martha Snow for that matter.

He was about to give up and continue on to Lydel Springs when someone suggested he try the cemetery. There was a man living out there, he was told, who knew ancestors, not to mention every name on every grave.

Hurricane's cemetery, like so many early burial grounds, sat high on a hill overlooking the townsite. The nearest structure, a flimsy shack fronted by a disintegrating picket fence, looked old enough to have survived from pioneer times. Only the flower garden out front made the place look lived in.

Traveler waited for the dust to settle around the Jeep before getting out. He'd been expecting an old-timer with whiskers. What he got was a young man with a blond crewcut who could have been this year's college freshman.

"I'm Dave Reynolds," he said, smiling, obviously delighted to have company. "You must be looking for your ancestors."

"Close."

"Or maybe you're a researcher like myself." He thoughtfully rubbed a hand over the spines of his crewcut. "If you'd come next week, I'd have been long gone. My job here is done."

"What's that exactly?"

"I'm surveying the graves as a part of my senior thesis at B.Y.U."

"You don't look that old."

"I'm twenty-one. I leave on my two-year mission right after graduation in June."

"You're the man to see, then. I'm trying to locate a family named Varney."

"They're here all right. Generations of them."

So far so good, Traveler thought. "What about Martha Ann Snow? I've been told she moved here from somewhere in Arizona."

"You're in luck. She's buried here, too."

Traveler blinked in surprise. "That's one grave I'd better see for myself."

"I've got the whole place charted. Just let me get my map."

Reynolds ducked back inside the shack and was out again in seconds, holding a paper the size of an architect's blueprint. Eagerly he spread it out on the Jeep's hood. After a moment, his finger stabbed a spot that looked to be in the northeast corner of the cemetery.

"I'll lead the way," he said. "Just watch where you step. Some of the markers are very fragile."

The dates for Martha Snow were 1901 to 1956.

"That's the right name," Traveler said, "but the wrong woman. It's probably the mother of the woman I'm looking for."

"How old is your subject?"

"About forty. The information I have is that she came to Hurricane to be married. She must have moved to Salt Lake soon after. I'm not sure of the dates, though it has to be at least twenty years ago."

"You aren't LDS, are you?"

Here we go again, Traveler thought, and showed the man his license. Dave Reynolds looked thrilled; he had never met a private detective before.

"I'll bet there's a crime involved."

"Murder." Traveler stretched the point somewhat despite the killing in Bountiful.

"Jeez. Maybe I can help. I know someone who goes back a long time in this part of the country. His name is Jess Dunphy. He's in his nineties now and can't get around much. But he's still sharp as a tack. I'll take you to see him."

Dunphy lived in a tiny aluminum-sided house at the edge of town. He looked the part of an old-timer, right down to the whiskers. At first he said he didn't remember a thing, but when Reynolds brought out a pint of bourbon, possession of which would have gotten him thrown out of B.Y.U., the man became talkative.

"Young Martha came from over near Lydel Springs

all right, came here to get married. Right then I knew there'd be trouble."

He paused to take a pull at the pint, his eyes bright. Traveler knew the look; the man wanted to be coaxed.

"What kind of trouble?" Traveler obliged.

After swallowing more bourbon Dunphy smacked his lips. "Folks from that part of the country are cursed. It goes back a long way, to the late eighteen sixties. In those days there was a tribe of Indians living where Lydel Springs is today. But us white men wanted the water and decided to get rid of them. Some say it was Brigham Young's Danites who did the job. Others claim it was local vigilantes."

The old man grinned at Dave Reynolds, who'd gone wide-eyed at the mention of his prophet. But the young man didn't say anything.

"Some of the Indians escaped the first ambush and took refuge on a mesa out in the desert. The place was impossible to climb and fight at the same time, so the white men just hunkered down to wait, intending to starve the heathens to death. When the braves realized they were beaten, they said their prayers and threw their women and children off the mountaintop to stop their suffering. After that they jumped, too. Those who saw it say the mountain turned red with blood. That place has been known as Blood Butte ever since. Those who live around Lydel Springs have never been the same, either."

Traveler dragged his chair closer to Dunphy. "Are you saying that Martha was cursed, too?"

"She's dead, ain't she?"

"Not in my cemetery," Reynolds said.

"You don't know everything, Davie." The old man

wet his whistle one more time. "She's out there, all right, next to her mother."

"There should be a marker," Reynolds complained.

"There wasn't money for that. Besides, folks wanted to keep it quiet."

"There's nothing on my chart," Reynolds persisted.

"They just came in one day, dug a hole, and put her to rest."

"Who did?" Traveler said.

"I was there myself," Dunphy said. "But then, I'm the last of the Zion Reborners left in these parts. The others cleared out after the burial."

"And you?" Traveler prompted.

"I'm too old to move and too old to give a damn about what I say, either. Let the chips fall where they may. That's my motto."

With that, he handed the bottle to Traveler, who took a small pull at it before returning it.

"I hope nobody minds if I kill this." Dunphy held up the pint to the light. He smiled at what he saw and drank. When he finished he sighed and closed his eyes.

For a moment Traveler thought the old man had nodded off. But his eyes popped open again and he went on with his tale. "The story they gave out was that Martha was killed in a fall from Blood Butte. But I ask you, why the hell would a woman her age be climbing up there? The answer's pretty damned obvious. She wouldn't. But nobody around here listens to me."

"I do," Traveler said.

The old man leaned forward until he was only inches from Traveler's face. There was a smell of dust about him, overshadowing the whiskey. "You wouldn't happen to have another bottle, would you?"

"I can go out and get you one."

"Do an old man a favor instead, will you? Leave a couple of dollars with Dave here. He'll take care of me."

The B.Y.U. scholar flushed with guilt.

Traveler handed the young man a twenty.

Dunphy grinned and continued. "Martha's husband was a man named Earl Jordan, a mean bastard at the best of times. When drinking he was even meaner. After she died there were whispers that Earl beat her to death and then repented to Brother Jacob. He was our leader, the First Prophet of the Church of Zion Reborn."

"You don't look like a believer."

"When a man gets to be my age, he believes in three squares a day. They fed me. I got down on my knees."

"What about Jacob?" Reynolds asked, a look of horrified fascination on his face, as if blasphemy were as titillating as forbidden sex.

"What I heard was that he helped Earl carry Martha's body up Blood Butte. They threw her off to make her injuries look like an accident. I can't prove that, you understand. But I believe it. Why the hell else do you think I stayed behind when the others left, just for my three squares?"

"The church takes care of you," Reynolds said.

Dunphy winked at Traveler. "Like I said, I go down on my knees when it suits me."

"Was there any kind of investigation?" Traveler asked.

"They called the sheriff out from Lydel Springs.

But what the hell could he do? There was Martha lying at the foot of Blood Butte and nobody to say it wasn't an accident. Right after that Jacob got his revelation from God. The only way to beat the Mormons, God told him, was to join them. Suffering out in the desert was a waste of time."

Dunphy paused to chuckle, which soon turned into a cough. He spit phlegm into a tin can next to his chair. " 'We'll move back to Salt Lake,' Jacob told us. 'We'll go into business and make money and be legitimate.' That was his word, *legitimate*."

The old-timer shook his head. "If you ask me, Brother Jacob finally figured out he couldn't get enough good-looking women to live out in the desert with him. Hellsakes, I could have told him that and saved God the trouble. The heat around here sucks a woman dry and shrivels her like a mummy. Take Martha. She didn't weigh much more than a mummy when they tossed her over the edge. If she had, they'd never have been able to carry her to the top, the bastards. Someone ought to make them pay."

"Jordan's dead," Traveler said. "Somebody killed him."

"Good riddance," Dunphy said and spit into his tin can for emphasis. "You being here wouldn't have anything to do with the woman who came to see me last week, would it?"

Traveler looked at Reynolds, who shrugged ignorance of such a visitor.

"Was she young?"

"Younger than I."

"Blond hair?"

"No such luck."

"Where can I find the Church of Zion Reborn now?"

Dunphy snorted. "That's just it. You can't. Brother Jacob said they were going underground, joining the church, pretending to pay full tithe, and all the while waiting for the day when they were strong enough to take over."

"Impossible," Reynolds said. "That's just whiskey talking."

"Maybe so, but then, you never did meet Brother Jacob."

"I'd like to," Traveler said.

"That ought to be easy enough. He's a dentist." The old man pulled out his dentures and held them up for inspection. "He made these for me."

18

A half hour later Traveler crossed the border into Arizona, where the long arm of the Mormon Church wasn't quite so effective. Neither was law and order.

By the time he reached Lydel Springs he was beginning to think that Hurricane had been a metropolis. A road sign said the population of the Arizona town was 1,200 but, judging by the number of houses visible, he figured the count at half that.

There was a single filling station, one bar, one market, an auto parts store, a sheriff's office, plus half a dozen forlorn-looking businesses on their way to bankruptcy.

The station, selling a brand of gasoline he'd never heard of, looked as if it might close at any moment. So he decided to fill the Jeep's tank, including the extra five-gallon can strapped on the back.

The grease-stained attendant, yawning constantly while he worked, made Traveler feel sleepy.

"I'm looking for Blood Butte," Traveler said.

"Shit," said the attendant, trying to spit but failing in the desert air. "If you're looking for the polygamists, they're long gone."

"I'm a tourist," Traveler said, wondering if he wasn't making the trip more out of morbid curiosity than anything else.

"Sure you are." The attendant squinted at him. "Just keep heading out the highway. You can't miss it. There's a junk car near the old dirt turnoff. You might still be able to smell the women for all I know."

"This turnoff, does it go all the way to the butte?"

"Yeah," the man said with an elaborate yawn. "But it's rough country out there. You might want to let the sheriff know you're making the trip. It'll save him trouble later on if you turn up missing."

About twenty miles outside of town, Traveler saw the marker, a rusting truck carcass that looked as if scavengers had picked it clean years ago. He swung the Jeep off the highway and onto what had once been a gravel road.

Immediately a tail of dust kicked up behind him like an exclamation point announcing his arrival. He slowed to five miles an hour but the dust didn't settle. At that speed, according to the directions he'd been given, it would take him an hour to reach the base of the butte. He pushed the Jeep to fifteen miles an hour and then held on as it bounced from one pothole to another.

He was heading almost directly east now, toward a thousand-foot slab of jagged sandstone that rose from the barren landscape like a prehistoric tomb. Closer around him, the desert floor was spotted with stunted shrubs and cactus, all eking out an existence in a rocky soil that looked as though it would eventually erode into pure sand. It was the kind of place, he thought, that only an angry God would create.

In the distance dust devils were sucking up enough sand to make them look like moving pillars of salt.

The sunlight faded abruptly and for the first time he noticed thunderheads gathering behind the stone monolith. The temperature dropped suddenly. The air smelled of ozone, as if lightning were about to strike.

He slowed the vehicle to a stop, eyeing the sinkhole ahead. From a distance it looked completely bleached of life, like an alkali flat.

Leaving the engine idling, he stepped outside to study the thunderheads. They were rolling toward him at breakneck speed, as if he were watching time-lapse photography.

He quickly climbed back inside, tightened his seat belt and shoulder harness, switched to four-wheel drive, and punched the accelerator. Flash floods were common in the desert and he sure as hell didn't want to be caught in a sinkhole.

The abandoned headquarters of the Church of Zion Reborn came into sight a few minutes later. Church was hardly an apt description. What he saw was a half-dozen shacks that looked as though they'd disintegrate if anyone made the mistake of leaning against them. One building in particular, an old barn, reminded him of a pile of bleached bones. All of the structures looked small, dwarfed as they were by Blood Butte.

The road ran out. There was no sign of life. Even so, he had the feeling that he was being watched, a sensation so strong he had to fight down an impulse to turn around and drive away.

In the end he ignored his instincts and stepped out of the Jeep. Even so, caution got the better of him; he carefully searched each of the buildings but found nothing except a few pieces of forsaken furniture.

As soon as he was outside again, lightning crackled. Thunder rolled over him a couple of seconds later. The sandstone butte creaked.

He stared up at the mountain. The sides were practically sheer, with no sign of footholds. A sheriff, even a small-town sheriff, should have realized that a middle-aged woman would have trouble with such a climb. Then again, how the hell could two men carry a body up that mountain?

He began walking along the base, looking for some kind of vertical access. Not more than a hundred yards from the barn he found a rock chimney of sorts, camouflaged by a fallen slab of rock. The opening angled up steeply. In places, steps had been cut in the sandstone, probably by nineteenth-century Indians judging by the amount of erosion on the treads.

Lightning, this time much closer, triggered thunder enough to bring a shower of red pebbles down on Traveler's head. He looked straight up. Directly overhead the sky was still blue. He decided to risk a short climb just to see if the old man's claims about Brother Jacob and Earl Jordan were possible.

The moment he touched the rock, he knew he had to be back down before it rained. Water would make the sandstone slippery and dangerous.

From the ground, he couldn't see more than twenty feet of chimney before it twisted out of sight. That twist was the turning point. After that, the climb was much easier. Two strong men would have no trouble carrying a woman's body. Whether they could make it all the way to the top was still to be proved. But they actually didn't have to get that far. A drop of a hundred feet or so, with the body bouncing from outcrop to outcrop, might do enough damage to hide the marks left by a man's fists.

At about that height Traveler reached a shallow cave that formed enough of a platform so that he could sit down. He took a deep breath. More than ever the desert air smelled like rain.

He was about to start down when an outcropping of sandstone exploded near his head. Shards of rock ripped open his cheek. An instant later the sound of the rifle shot arrived, a more deadly kind of thunder.

He rolled to the back of the cave. Even there he was only a few feet from the edge of the butte. He felt helpless. The .45 in his hand was good only for close-in work.

Another shot dug sandstone from the red wall above him. A persistent sniper with enough ammunition could probably undermine the entire ledge if he were a good enough marksman.

Thunder shook the mountain. With it came the rain, a sheet of water that sluiced down the mountainside, forming a curtain between Traveler and the sniper.

Traveler eased forward until he could cover the chimney approach, just in case the sniper might be foolish enough to try finishing the job in person. The movement started him sliding headfirst on the wet sandstone. He caught himself just in time. With such treacherous footing no one would be coming after him. He wasn't going anywhere either.

A short time later, the rain stopped as abruptly as it had begun. The sun came out. Steam rose from the drying rock. But Traveler waited for darkness before climbing down. By then he was angry enough to hope the sniper was still waiting. But the descent was uneventful. The Jeep was right where he left it, untouched except for a coating of mud that looked like dried blood.

He wore out a set of flashlight batteries looking for footprints and cartridge casings. But the rain had washed everything away.

19

There was only one place open in Lydel Springs after dark, the Silver Spur Bar and Grill. Even the sheriff's office was closed, though there was an emergency telephone number pasted on the door.

Traveler parked in front of the bar and switched on the Jeep's overhead light. For a moment he just sat there, staring down at his filthy clothes. Finally he took a deep breath and began slapping at them violently. Most of the crusted mud disintegrated into dust, though the red stain remained.

He studied his face in the rearview mirror. More than spit would be needed to make it acceptable.

He opened the door and got out. Country music came from inside the bar, the same kind Claire liked. Maybe his mind wanted to escape the shooting at Blood Butte; maybe the implications of attempted murder were too much to deal with in his exhausted state. Whatever the case, his memory played tricks. That last night with Claire came back all too vividly.

"I've been lost my entire life," she'd told him in that vulnerable moment following orgasm. "But you're the first one I've ever asked to find me."

He'd still been inside her then, though shrinking away rapidly.

"Right now, with you like this," she'd whispered in his ear, "is the only time I don't feel forgotten. Can you do it again?"

"I'm not as young as I used to be."

"Here. Let me help." She went to work with a vengeance.

"Someday I want to die like this," she'd gasped a little while later. "With you leading me out of my darkness."

With an effort of will he shook himself free of the recollection and went inside. After washing the best he could with cold water and no soap, Traveler closed himself in an old-fashioned phone booth. He called his father first but got no answer. After that, he dialed his answering service. Willis Tanner had called once, asking for a status report as soon as possible. Claire had also phoned. Her message, as read back to him, was: "In our game of hide-and-seek, you'll always be *it*."

He found an opening at the bar and was looking over the Silver Spur's half-dozen customers, searching for a law enforcement-type face, when one of the drinkers, a beefy man wearing a baseball cap with a Budweiser logo stitched on the front, pointed at him and said, "Hey, I know you. Didn't you play linebacker for L.A.?"

Traveler nodded.

The man slapped one of his buddies on the back. "Shit, yes. This here is Moroni Traveler. He was one mean mother-fucker." He pointed a finger at Traveler. "Man, I loved watching you on *Monday Night Football*. Hell, I remember Howard Cosell talking about

146

your eyes. Linebackers have crazy eyes, he said, but yours were the craziest of all. Goddamn, that was great, watching a homegrown Utah boy clobber those nigger running backs."

"You're damn right," said the guy who'd had his back pounded. "Football used to be a white man's sport. Say, whatever happened to you, anyway?"

Traveler ignored the question and ordered a beer.

"What was it, a knee?"

The first man, the back-slapper, smacked his own thigh and said, "No, by God. I remember now. You broke some guy's neck. The poor gazooney ended up like a vegetable being rolled around in a wheelchair."

Perfect, Traveler thought. This was exactly why he stayed out of bars. They were always full of good old boys who had nothing better to do than relive his past. For them it was vicarious excitement; for him it was a reminder of a darker side of himself that was better left forgotten.

"The gazooney played for Pittsburgh, didn't he?"

"That's right," someone chimed in.

Pittsburgh, Traveler thought, feeling himself slip back into the dressing room one more time. Ankles and wrists taped, pads in place, tugging on the skin-tight silver uniform that gave you that foolish illusion of being invulnerable.

And all the while the coach was working on him. "That goddamned Jack Ensor caught seven passes against us last time. Seven for a hundred and twenty yards. He killed us. Do you hear me, Traveler? Four of those catches were over the middle. Your area of responsibility. Have you got that?"

He nodded.

"I don't expect miracles, goddammit. He's going to catch a few, no doubt about it. But when he does, you make the son of a bitch pay. Hit him so hard he'll think twice the next time."

"Make him pay," the defensive backs chorused.

When the pep talk ended, Mel Jensen, Traveler's roommate on the road, went into his usual pregame routine. "Goddammit, Traveler, come over here. I'm going to put my indelible mark on you." He had one of those self-inking rubber stamps, one with a skull and crossbones.

Playing his part, Traveler approached with mock servility.

Jensen stamped him high on the forehead where Pete Rozelle wouldn't see it, even on instant replays.

"That makes you our middle-deathbacker," Jensen pronounced.

Everybody laughed except the coach, who shouted, "That's right. Anybody comes over the middle on a crossing pattern, Traveler, kill the fucker."

The back-slapper pulled his baseball cap down over his eyes and tugged at his belt. "Seeing you here in person, without all those fancy TV cameras and lights, you don't look so tough to me."

At that, the group at the bar surged forward until they'd surrounded Traveler and his heckler. "I had some trouble out at Blood Butte," Traveler told them.

"You can't trust what you see on TV," his tormentor persisted.

"Maybe I ought to talk to the sheriff," Traveler responded, refusing to meet the man's stare.

But the heckler, obviously seeing himself as a self-appointed spokesman, poked a finger against Traveler's chest. "You're a has-been. You're history."

Here it comes, Traveler thought. They weren't going to let him back away. His breathing changed. His eyes lost focus as he stoked himself with anger, the same way he'd gotten ready for the big games.

Without looking at his hands, he knew they'd be trembling slightly. His eyes would be changing, too. Probably something to do with adrenaline. Whatever it was, it had made him an all-pro. It also kept him from recognizing his own face on videotape replays.

The man in the Budweiser hat must have seen something, too, because he abruptly backed off, his aggression melting away like ice exposed to sudden flame.

His friend said, "Jesus Christ, I just remembered something else. It was in the papers at the time. This guy quit football because it made him crazy. He was afraid he'd kill someone."

The bartender said, "Okay, fellas. That does it. I'm closing up for the night."

"Linebacker's eyes," someone muttered. "He's still got 'em."

"Out," said the bartender.

The Budweiser hat led the exodus.

Unsteadily Traveler guided his beer to his lips and swallowed.

"That includes you, too," the bartender said.

"Where can I find the sheriff?" he said.

"Complaining won't do you a damn bit of good. Cyrus Taylor drinks here like everybody else in town."

20

Sheriff Taylor didn't like being roused out of bed in the middle of the night. But he did invite Traveler inside when he heard that someone had tried to kill him out at Blood Butte.

"It wouldn't be the first time there'd be a murder out there, you know." The sheriff led the way into the kitchen where he put a kettle on to boil. "I'll make us some decaffeinated coffee, though why I bother with the damn stuff I don't know. It still keeps me awake."

The sheriff turned from the stove and chuckled. "I know what you're thinking. I don't look old enough for this job. The fact is, I got elected right out of junior college. Of course, nobody else was running."

Traveler studied the sheriff. He couldn't have been more than thirty. There were no lines in his tanned face, and he was still lean enough to wear jeans without looking like he'd been stuffed into them by a taxidermist.

"For several years," the sheriff said, "we had screwballs homesteading out at Blood Butte. Religion fanatics practicing polygamy and God knows what."

"Blood atonement?"

"Could be. But they finally moved out, lock, stock, and barrel. There's nobody left out there to shoot at you. Could have been a sheepherder taking target practice."

"I was the target. Take my word for it."

"I can go out tomorrow morning and take a look around. But after that rain I probably won't find a damned thing."

"I'll settle for some information about Brother Jacob."

"Shit. I should have known. That bastard used to be our dentist here in town. Of course, that was before he started talking to God. In person." Sheriff Taylor chuckled at the memory. "At first people felt sorry for him. Later on he started scaring the piss out of everybody, me included."

"What happened?"

"It started when he got himself lost in the desert. He was missing for days. We kept sending out search parties long after we figured he was a goner. We were about to give up when he stumbled out of the wilderness half dead, saying God had spoken just like He had to Moses. He said God gave him the word on polygamy."

A wide grin made the sheriff look younger than ever. "His wife went absolutely nuts, I can tell you. She up and left him as soon as he started putting his new religion into practice."

He stopped talking long enough to add instant coffee to the pot of boiling water. "After that there was a lot of talk in town about burning Jacob out. But the plain fact is people around here were afraid to go up against him out there at Blood Butte.''

"And you, Sheriff?''

"I said a prayer of thanks the day he and his followers up and left town." He poured coffee into heavy china mugs, adding milk and sugar without consulting Traveler.

"That was right after Martha Snow was killed, wasn't it?''

"Is that why you're here?''

Traveler nodded.

"Some woman called me looking for her a while back.''

"That must have been her daughter.''

The sheriff shrugged. "I thought she was a reporter. We've had too many of them around here already. So I told her I'd never heard of anyone by that name. It was only a little lie, since old Martha was calling herself Sister Jordan when I knew her.''

"Her husband is John Varney, an important man in the LDS church.''

"Jesus Christ. Nobody told me that.''

"There was no divorce. At best she was Earl Jordan's common-law wife.''

"That's all I need, trouble with the Mormons.''

"Maybe I can head it off if you give me enough information.''

"There was nothing I could do. They showed me her body. There were twenty-five witnesses ready to swear they saw her fall from the butte. Jacob's witnesses to be sure, but witnesses nevertheless.''

"So you swept it under the rug?''

"Hell no. We had a proper inquest before I let Jacob and his people take off. The verdict was accidental death. It could have been worse."

"How?"

"It could have been suicide."

21

Promptly at nine o'clock the next morning Traveler called the downtown office of Dr. Jake Ruland.

"Good morning," Penny said. Her voice tinkled cheerfully. "May I help you smile?"

"I'd like to make an appointment to see Dr. Ruland."

"Personally."

"Yes, indeed."

"Mr. Traveler, is that you?"

"I want you to pretend that I'm a regular patient. Don't tell him I want to see him as a detective."

"I don't know if I can do that. Doctor has fifty other dentists working for him. He seldom sees new patients himself, unless they're young women." She tried to make light of that by laughing.

"I'm tired. I drove most of the night to get here. Once I did I couldn't sleep worth a damn." Though he did dream about snipers and a sandstone mountain that leaked blood, but he didn't tell her that.

"I can hear it in your voice. You found out something about my mother."

"We'll talk about that after I see Dr. Jake."

"What does he have to do with it?"

"You tell me. You're the one working for him."

"A personal appointment with Dr. Ruland involves an additional charge." Penny's voice had gone cold, as if the conversation were suddenly being overheard.

"That's fine," he said, playing along. "The sooner the better."

"We can squeeze you in just before noon, eleven forty-five. Please be on time."

Dr. Ruland's office was decorated in shades of gray and maroon, with a louver window that opened out onto Main Street. The dental chair, covered in a tweedy material that again mixed gray and maroon, was camouflaged to look like a living-room recliner. Drills and other instruments were nowhere to be seen. No doubt they'd been carefully hidden away in the cherrywood cabinets designed to resemble end tables. But the antiseptic smell hadn't changed since Traveler's childhood.

A dental hygienist, flaunting her white smile, sat him down and attached his bib. "Doctor will be here in a minute."

He involuntarily clenched his teeth.

She smiled, took up a dental mirror and pick. "Time for a preliminary look. We don't want to waste doctor's time once he gets here."

Two hundred and fifty dollars a day wasn't enough, he thought, and opened wide.

While she probed and scraped, he stared at the clear blue sky beyond the window and wondered if the forecasters were right, if another storm really was on its way. They'd already dubbed it Yukon Junior.

The hygienist had just begun to suction excess saliva when Dr. Ruland's bearded face blotted out the view. In his hand he had the patient card Traveler had filled out a few minutes before. Behind him, leading against the wall, arms folded across his chest, stood Brother Lehi. His smile was that of a saint welcoming martyrdom.

"I'm glad to see that Penny is recommending me to her friends," Ruland said.

"Actually," Traveler said, "I'm here on business."

The dentist nodded at his hygienist. "All right, Sue, I'll take things from here."

The young woman looked questioningly at Traveler, but left without a word.

The moment she was gone the dentist said, "You're a private detective, aren't you?"

"Is that what Penny told you?"

"She didn't have to. I know she's been looking for someone to help locate her mother." Ruland smiled, obviously pleased with himself. "Your teeth need cleaning, Mr. Traveler. I hope my girl told you that."

"You have a strange kind of logic, Doctor. Why would a private detective working for Penny come looking for you?"

"I'm sure you'll tell me."

Traveler spoke casually. "I've just come back from Blood Butte."

Ruland showed no surprise. "No doubt you've been talking to Jess Dunphy. I wouldn't believe everything an old man like that tells you."

"And the Church of Zion Reborn?"

Lehi chuckled.

"That's all behind me now," Ruland said. "I have seen the light and come back to the true church. I have received my endowments in the temple. I follow the old-fashioned ways. I wear my garments at all times."

He was referring to a kind of holy underclothes, complete with embroidered mystic signs. Originally, Mormon garments had resembled union suits. These days, however, they were abbreviated for modern living. The truly devout still wore them continuously, even to bathe, accomplishing that feat by dangling garment-clad arms or legs from shower or tub.

"Why didn't you tell Penny that her mother is dead?"

"Her mother came to us as Martha Varney, not Snow. Isn't that right, Brother Lehi?"

The acolyte nodded.

Ruland continued, "I didn't take the connection at first. By the time I did, I couldn't bring myself to hurt the child."

"She's no child. And you don't treat her like one, either."

"I feel a duty to protect her, probably because I failed her mother."

"In what way?"

"I could have prevented her liaison with Earl Jordan."

"Did he come back to the *true* church with you?"

"Who knows what's in a man's heart?" Ruland lowered his head as if in prayer. "As for Martha, only Earl knew the truth of what drove her to jump from Blood Butte. And now he's dead, too."

"Are you claiming that Martha killed herself?"

"For Penny's sake, I don't claim anything."

"There are those who say the Church of Zion isn't dead, that it's gone underground here in Salt Lake."

Ruland laughed. "Jess Dunphy again. I loved that man once. I should never have left him behind unattended. Drink has gotten hold of him."

"Maybe you did leave someone behind." Traveler was thinking of Dave Reynolds, who may have only been pretending to do graveyard research for B.Y.U.

Ruland shook a finger at the detective, the gesture of a long-suffering parent rebuking an unruly child. "You can't trap me that way, Mr. Traveler. I have the innocence of one reborn in Christ."

"How does the church stand on blood atonement these days? My blood in particular."

"Only a fool would fail to heed God's warning. But don't look at me. I had three crowns and two extractions yesterday. I didn't even have time for lunch."

"Can you say the same for the rest of your flock?" Traveler stared at Lehi.

The little man pushed slowly away from the wall. When he spoke, a half smile remained fixed in place. His mad eyes were the equal of Charles Manson's. "Brother Ruland calls me his littlest angel." He made a face at Traveler's bulk. "Being small has its advantages. Natural camouflage, I call it. It won me medals in 'Nam."

"Infantry?"

"Special Forces. Sniper. When I fire at something I hit it. Unless of course I want to miss."

"Like at Blood Butte?"

Ruland put an arm around Traveler's shoulder, easing him toward the door as he spoke. "Have you read *The Book of Mormon?*"

"On occasion."

"Mormon, eight: forty-one, Mr. Traveler. 'Behold, the sword of vengeance hangeth over you; and the time soon cometh that he avengeth the blood of the saints upon you.' "

22

The old snow was just starting to go slushy underfoot as Traveler and Penny walked north on Main Street. Ahead of them stood Brigham Young's statue, his back forever to the temple, one hand stretched out toward a local bank.

"Typical of him," Penny said.

"Don't be too hard on the old boy. To succeed in this desert he had to be a pragmatist."

Temple Square was to their left. Beyond, toward the Great Salt Lake, was a line of black clouds as solid as a mountain range.

"We'd better get inside somewhere," Traveler suggested.

Penny stopped on the sidewalk and stood on tiptoe to peer into his face. "It's bad news, isn't it?" Her eyes glistened, foreshadowing tears. "I think I've known it all along, ever since the letters stopped coming."

Traveler glanced around, looking for someplace more private. He dismissed the ZCMI, the Zion's Cooperative Mercantile Institution, a pioneer attempt by the church to boycott gentile merchants. More recently it had become a shopping mall dedicated to profit rather than faith.

"Come on." He took her by the arm and led her across South Temple toward the Hotel Utah. To Traveler, the hotel's ten stories of white terra-cotta brick always seemed cheerful, much more of a beacon than the gray granite facade of the temple on the other side of the street.

The hotel, in the ornate style of the French Renaissance, had been built by the church in 1911. An elaborate cupola in the shape of the state emblem, the beehive, graced the top.

They went inside. The lobby was lavish, with marble pillars and floors, and cornices of elegantly carved wooden scrollwork. The beehive emblem was repeated in plush rugs and elaborate mosaics. Once there had been a bar in the lobby, cause of a religious ruckus back when the place first opened. Although liquor is Satan's work to Mormons, the leader of the church at the time, Joseph Fielding Smith, said business is business. If visitors to the city couldn't get something to drink at the Hotel Utah they'd stay somewhere else. But following World War II, pragmatism gave way to fervor and liquor was banished forever. As a result the hotel was now losing money, also a sin in the Mormon scheme of things. For that reason the ten-story building, which stands in the shadow of the temple, was soon to be converted into additional office space for the church.

"I think we both need a drink," Traveler said, aware of more than one bootlegging bellboy.

Penny's head twitched. "I can't go back to work smelling like that."

Traveler led her to a remote corner of the lobby, where they sat side by side in straight-backed chairs. The tears that had threatened were now a reality. He offered her his wadded handkerchief but she opted for tissues from her purse.

"I found her grave," he said gently.

She gasped. Her hands began to shake, then her entire body. She panted, trying to recover her breath, but couldn't seem to make her lungs work. Finally she doubled over until her head was nearly touching her knees.

Traveler stroked her back. The sounds coming from her changed, half retch, half gasp.

"I'm sorry," he said, his words sounding ridiculously inadequate.

She moaned softly and raised up far enough for him to see tears streaming down her cheeks. "How?"

"I don't know for sure. I talked to an old man who knew her, and to the sheriff. Neither was an eyewitness."

A sigh escaped her, long and drawn out, like the ending of life. "Is it nice, her resting place?"

He thought of the bleak desert burial ground, the unmarked grave. "It overlooks the town where your ancestors were born."

She lurched to her feet. When he started to stand she waved him back into his chair.

"Excuse me," she said, and rushed toward the ladies' room before he could say a word.

She returned ten minutes later, a wad of tissues clutched in one hand. Her face looked composed except for red-rimmed, swollen eyes.

"When did Mother pass over?"

"A year ago, I think." About the time Brother Jacob went through a metamorphosis to become Dr. Jake, he added to himself. "I can get you the exact date if you want it."

Traveler watched her face. "She may have been murdered," he added.

Breath left her again. She began shaking worse than before. Maybe her job with Jake Ruland was a coincidence after all.

For a moment he thought she might have to retreat to the ladies' room again, but she managed to calm herself. Even so, he waited a full minute more before asking, "Why are you working for Jake Ruland?"

"I heard my father talking about him, how he'd once been the leader of the Church of Zion Reborn." Her voice was scratchy with strain. "I thought if I got to know Dr. Jake, I might come to understand my mother's motives. The Mormon Church was no longer acceptable to me. I went looking for something better. What I found was Dr. Jake's First Conclave."

Traveler thought he'd heard just about everything LDS, but this was something new. His mystified look prompted Penny to add, "The First Conclave coincides with territory around Dr. Jake's downtown office. Each of his offices has its own conclave."

"Are they sanctioned by the church?"

"Of course not," she said, trying unsuccessfully to sound indignant. "I wouldn't have joined otherwise."

"How many offices are there?"

"Twenty-five at the moment. Eventually Jake hopes to establish one conclave to coincide with each LDS ward."

"Does your father know about this?"

"I hope not. I want it to be a surprise when Jake finally makes his move."

"What move is that?"

Penny tried to smile. The expression looked absurd on her anguished face. "As far as I'm concerned, my father is an accomplice to murder. He drove my mother away. If he hadn't she'd still be alive. He and his religious intolerance exiled her into the wilderness. From that moment on I ceased being LDS in my heart." Her voice caught and she had to swallow several times before continuing. "The church should be pulled down stone by stone."

"And you see Dr. Jake as the one to do it?"

"Why not?"

"He may have tried to cover up your mother's death." Traveler went on to recount Jess Dunphy's story of collusion between Earl Jordan and Jake Ruland, who was then Brother Jacob. "That's only hearsay, of course."

"Dear God." Her eyes closed, removing the only touch of color from her dead-white face. "Do you think it's true?"

"I think it's convenient that the man being accused of the actual crime is dead and can't defend himself."

"If Jordan didn't do it, who did?"

He was about to suggest the person who shot at him, but she spoke first, a hoarse whisper. "You think it was Dr. Jake, don't you?" Her eyes opened wide.

"I'd be very careful of him if I were you."

"That can't be. I . . . he's not that kind of man. If you knew more about him, you'd understand."

"Tell me about him, then?"

She shook her head. "It's better that you find out

for yourself. All you have to do is go to one of his conclaves around closing time and give the password. Just say 'I'm from Nauvoo,' and you'll be enlightened."

Traveler thought that over for a moment. "There's something else. I've heard speculation that your mother killed herself."

"I don't believe it."

"I climbed partway up that damned mesa. It's not the kind of place I'd choose to jump from."

"Nor would my mother. She was terrified of heights."

"Your dentist friend says otherwise."

"He would say something like that rather than speak ill of the dead, even about a man like Earl Jordan."

"I think you're being naive."

"You don't know him like I do."

"Enlighten me."

"He's asked me to marry him in the temple." She tried to laugh but couldn't manage it. "The church thinks he's only a black bishop."

"He's using you, Penny."

"You've missed the point. I'm using him to get back at my father."

"And if he helped Earl Jordan?"

"Then I'll find out about it. You see, Mr. Traveler, there are few secrets in a dental office. And none at all in bed. Only last night I learned that Dr. Jake is planning something special for the church, and with a relative of mine at that."

"What are you saying?"

"He and Reuben Dixon are this close." She held up crossed fingers.

"And?" he probed.

"I don't know, yet."

Traveler took a deep breath, letting it out slowly as he stared at Penny. When she'd first entered his office he'd mistaken her for a twenty-year-old. Now he knew better. She'd squandered her youth a long time ago.

His eyes burned with lack of sleep. "You hired me to find your mother," he said, standing up. "I've done that. I'll mail you an itemized list of expenses as soon as I can."

"Send it to my father. He'll pay just to keep you quiet."

23

Snow was falling by the time Traveler reached the Chester Building. Yukon Junior was living up to its billing, hiding the city's tainted slush beneath a fresh white shroud.

Traveler eased through the revolving door. The lobby's marble floor was slick and treacherous. He picked his way over to the cigar stand, where Barney Chester was reading the latest copy of the *Ensign*, the official church magazine.

"Someone claims to have actually discovered the remains of the Garden of Eden in Missouri," he said.

"I've been there," Traveler said. "There aren't any apple trees."

"A good point." Barney tossed the magazine under the counter with the pornography. They both knew that Joseph Smith had once revealed Independence, Missouri, as the site of the Garden of Eden. "Your sublet tenants have been stinking up the building."

"Bill and Charlie don't smell that bad."

"Who's talking sweat? One whiff of whatever they've been smoking and Brigham Young would turn over in his grave."

"I'll talk to them about it."

"I already did. Charlie says it's part of his religion."

"And Bill?"

Barney fired up a cigar and drew on it like a longtime addict. "He tells me he talks to God every time he inhales."

"It's snowing again. We can't send them out in the cold."

"I already did. Knowing them, they'll be back."

"Can you open up for me? I gave them my keys."

Barney sighed. "I wish you wouldn't do that." After another sigh he handed over a master key.

Nephi Bates, the building's only elevator operator, was on duty for the first time in days. As always, his face was pinched with disapproval at the smell of the tobacco smoke lingering on Traveler. He claimed to be named for Nephi in *The Book of Mormon*. He came from the town of the same name in southern Utah.

He sprayed deodorizer in the elevator just before the doors closed. Once the car started moving he said, "Willis Tanner told me to have you call him."

"You really are a spy, aren't you?"

"Mr. Tanner was here just a few minutes ago."

"Barney didn't say anything about it."

Bates pursed his lips. "Mr. Chester was in the basement checking the furnace." His tone implied that Barney's momentary absence had been ordained.

"Thank you." Traveler stepped out on the top floor. Bates followed him into the corridor, staying there on watch until Traveler entered his office.

Traveler had intended to call Tanner anyway and was put right through, avoiding the usual holding pattern with its Mormon Tabernacle Choir Muzak.

"What have you got to report?" Tanner asked immediately.

"Mission accomplished."

"You found the girl's mother?"

"Her grave."

"I see." Tanner didn't sound particularly surprised. "What now?"

"I'm without a client. Two, I guess. I certainly can't keep an eye on Penny if I'm no longer working for her."

"There's more than just the girl involved here."

"You admit that, do you?"

"I arranged police cooperation, didn't I? Now tell me what else you've got."

"Not what you want to hear. I found a witness who says the Varney woman was killed by Earl Jordan, most likely the result of a domestic quarrel. Could be that Brother Jacob, alias Dr. Jake Ruland, helped cover up the crime. But there's no proof."

"And the Church of Zion Reborn?"

"Long gone from Arizona, as if you didn't know with that intelligence system of yours. I hope you give Nephi Bates a break on his tithe."

"Doctrine and Covenants, Mo. 'He that is tithed shall not be burned at his coming.' "

"I haven't started spending your money yet, Willis. Do you want it back? Or should I keep poking around?"

"Do you have anything in mind?"

"I think the Varney girl could be in trouble."

"What kind?"

"I consider that privileged information."

"What are you saying, that you'd like to keep watching her?"

"And a few other things."

"I'll get back to you." Tanner hung up.

Traveler was still waiting for a return call when Mad Bill and Charlie arrived. The Indian produced an antique opium pipe from beneath his shirt and began packing it with a tobaccolike mixture.

"We liberated the pipe from the Era Antique Shop," Bill said. "But I actually paid for this." He rattled a brown grocery bag before reaching inside and extracting a handful of battered postcards. He thumbed through them until he came to one that looked like an old daguerreotype. He handed it to Traveler. "Look at those pioneer faces. People in those days had faith. You can see it in their eyes."

The next postcard, yellowed with age, its stamp torn away, showed a dour-looking Brigham Young surrounded by all twenty-seven of his wives.

"There was a man who had it made," Bill said. "All those willing women. They practically fell into his lap when Joe Smith was murdered. But me, I can't even find one."

"Maybe if you had a regular job," Traveler suggested.

"I do God's work."

Charlie snapped his fingers. "That's why."

"Why what?" Bill said, looking startled.

"Why he killed Joe Smith. To get the women."

Bill slapped the Indian on the back. "Not bad, Charlie. I can use it in one of my sermons."

Traveler shook his head. "You're not still on that old wives' tale, are you, Bill?"

"The end justifies the means. Anything to bring down the church."

For years Bill had been harping on apocryphal stories surrounding the murder of Joseph Smith, in particular one that said Brigham Young was behind the whole thing, not Freemasons as history reported.

"At the time of the killing," Bill picked up, "Brigham was already four years older than Smith, with little chance of ever coming to power on his own. Add to that the fact that Joe Smith, by his own admission, was a ladies' man, and Brigham had to be chafing at the bit. I mean, the women he had to choose from must have been leftovers."

Charlie struck a match and held it to the opium pipe, puffing quickly to get it going. The smoke reminded Traveler of burning hair.

Charlie filled his lungs before passing the pipe to Bill, who immediately inhaled deeply, holding the smoke inside for a long time. When he finally exhaled, his facial muscles lost all tension. The result was the serene look of an idiot. "Wouldn't it be something for a detective like you to solve a hundred-and-fifty-year-old murder."

"Whatever you're smoking," Traveler said, "is making me dizzy." He stepped to the window and jerked it open. A north wind blew in his face.

"You're destroying our fug," Bill moaned.

Traveler glanced over his shoulder to see Charlie and Bill huddling together, their foreheads touching like soldiers hoarding a match. Pipe smoke was drifting toward the door. The stench would soon reach the hallway.

Traveler slammed the window shut. His dizziness returned immediately.

One after the other, Bill and Charlie blew smoke at him.

"Breathe deeply," the Indian said. "You'll see God."

What Traveler saw, in his mind's eye at least, was Reuben Dixon, documents dealer. He, like Bill, had been talking about a pioneer murder at their last meeting. Had he come up with a document that would turn the old wives' tales into reality?

Traveler shook his head at such an idea. It didn't make sense. Dixon himself said John Varney had taken a pass on the buy. Surely nobody in the church would gamble like that, even with a counterfeit.

24

Willis Tanner arrived unannounced. He took one whiff, pointed a finger at Mad Bill, and said, "I'm calling the police in sixty seconds."

Bill's head swiveled toward Traveler, who said, "I'm surprised that one of the saints would have enough experience to recognize an illegal substance."

Tanner turned his finger on Charlie Redwine.

"The police don't bother me," the Indian said. "I come under federal jurisdiction."

"Thirty seconds." Tanner slowly brought his arm up to face level so that he could keep an eye on his wristwatch.

Bill squared his shoulders. "We'll be in the lobby if you need us, Moroni."

With that, he and Charlie exited, leaving a trail of smoke behind them.

The moment the office door closed behind them Tanner said, "What the hell were they smoking?"

"Some concoction of Charlie's. They can't afford anything too dangerous."

Waving one hand in front of his face, Tanner went to the window and attempted to open it. "It's stuck," he said, his face changing color because he was holding his breath.

When Traveler tried the window it opened easily enough.

"I must have loosened it," Tanner said, thrusting his head out into the cold air.

"You could have phoned."

Tanner didn't answer but merely exaggerated his breathing to show displeasure at having sinned by proxy. That went on for a full minute before the cold started him shaking. Only then did he pull his head back inside.

"I cannot speak the prophet's words in here. The air is tainted."

"Fine. Go out in the hall and shout them through the door."

"This is no joke, Moroni."

"I'm tired. I've driven from one end of the state to the other, I've been shot at, I've—"

"Shot at?"

Traveler briefly outlined his meeting with Jess Dunphy and what happened later at Blood Butte.

Throughout the explanation Tanner pulled at his chin like an old man feeling for whiskers. "Our prophet is right, then. He said one of his Moronis— you—would lead the way by exposing those who would desecrate our heritage."

"Willis, it's time you told me everything you know about the Church of Zion Reborn."

"Elton Woolley trusts you. He told me that himself. He said, 'Willis, go to him, our messenger. Tell him that he must keep watching.' Then he read from the Book. 'And it came to pass that Moroni sent spies into

174

the wilderness to watch their camp.' And now you, Moroni, will be the prophet's spy.''

"Why don't I just give you your money back and we'll call it quits?"

"Do this for us, Mo, and we'll owe you."

"I wish you'd put that in writing."

25

Snow from Yukon Junior didn't have the staying power of its predecessor. It was melting as soon as it struck asphalt, leaving the streets slick but passable.

Traveler, aware of his fatigue, drove slowly. The snow swirling against the windshield had a hypnotic effect. He rolled down the window, using the cold air to keep himself awake. By the time he reached home he was shivering uncontrollably.

His father hugged him at the door before backing off a step. "You look terrible."

"Not as bad as I feel." Traveler headed for the bathroom. "I need a hot bath."

While the tub filled Traveler told his father about the last twenty-four hours. When it came to the shooting, Martin, who'd been perched on the toilet seat, lunged to his feet. "Goddammit! That settles it. Will Tanner can get someone else."

"The girl is in over her head," Traveler said before submerging up to his neck in hot water. "She needs help."

"Maybe it's time I told you about your mother and me, about what women can do to you."

"I'm not planning to marry her."

Traveler submerged all the way for a moment. When he surfaced Martin said, "All right. We won't talk women right now. Besides which, I never walked away from a case once I'd taken it, so why should you?" The old man sat down with a groan, both hands clutching at the small of his back. "Growing old is not fun."

"When all this is over, I'll want to hear that story about you and Mother."

"At my age memory starts to go. Who's to say what I'll remember tomorrow, let alone next week?"

"Can you hold yourself together long enough to give me some help?"

Martin leaned toward the tub to stare his son straight in the eye. "Do you really want me to?"

"It's vital."

The old man nodded, a spreading grin slowly rearranged his face. "My arthritis only acts up in bad weather. It's nothing to worry about."

"Good. We'll wait until the sun goes down and tackle Reuben Dixon. He'll feel less secure in the dark."

Martin nodded. "That still gives you enough time to take a nap."

Traveler rose from the water. "I've got to have my teeth checked first."

Dr. Jake's cardboard alter ego was standing outside in the snow when Traveler arrived at the credit dentist's university branch. The receptionist, whose teeth were almost as bright as Penny's, said, "Good afternoon. May I help you smile?"

"I'm from Nauvoo," he said, ready to fake a tooth-ache should Penny's password fail.

"Of course, sir. Take a seat. We'll be closing in just a few minutes."

The waiting room was separate from the reception area. Its walls were pale green, so was the carpet. Chairs and sofas, done in a knubby material that mixed that same green with an earthy brown, lined three walls. A huge television screen, one of those projection models, took up the fourth wall. Programming came from a videotape deck and showed aquarium fish swimming lazily, accompanied by soft music.

He counted heads. There were a dozen seated around the room, all women. Traveler sat beside a middle-aged lady with swollen chipmunk cheeks. She inspected him openly. Like most of the others in the room she was overweight, much of it in her matronly bosom.

"We don't get many men in this conclave," she said, her tone heading toward condemnation. "Not during working hours anyway."

He smiled, trying to look sympathetic, and touched his cheeks where her own were so puffy.

"Oh, I'm in no pain. I had my wisdom teeth out last week. It takes forever for the swelling to go down. I'm here for the prayer meeting." As soon as the words were out she looked stricken. "Oh, dear. I'm not supposed to say things like that unless I'm certain about someone."

"I'm from Nauvoo," he whispered in her ear.

She sighed. "That's all right, then."

"I also have a bad tooth," he added, to keep the

conversation going. That way, at least, he would be less conspicuous.

She reached out shyly to pat his hand. "There's no worse pain, is there?"

Traveler obliged with a grimace.

"Don't worry. It's almost time. Then Dr. Jake can comfort you."

She left her chair to consult with a woman who occupied the chair nearest the tape deck. The second woman, who appeared to be heading into middle age at the rate of ten pounds a year, stared at Traveler and then at the clock. Traveler's new acquaintance whispered something and they both giggled. They were still at it when a bell sounded.

A moment later the receptionist came in. "It's all clear."

Faces lit up around the room.

The woman next to the videotape machine pushed a button. The fish disappeared. She quickly loaded another cassette and pushed the playback button. Organ music filled the room.

The first woman, her swollen cheeks quivering, hurried back to her chair at Traveler's side. She took his hand and said, "My name is Melba."

The television screen flared to life, showing earth as seen from outer space. The picture remained static for a moment before the camera zoomed toward the planet. Suddenly clouds engulfed everything. The music softened. A voice said, "God is at our door. We must answer with prayer."

Those in the waiting room eased from their seats and onto their knees, their eyes never leaving the television screen. Traveler mimicked their every move.

The clouds dissolved to reveal Jake Ruland. For a moment Traveler thought the man was wearing one of his white dental smocks. Then the camera moved back far enough to show a full-length robe. In one hand, Dr. Jake held a book. He opened it and read, " 'And the tempter came among us, bringing with him a contagion whose name was money. His guile was like the serpent. His words were honey.' "

"Amen," Melba said, squeezing Traveler's hand.

Ruland continued. " 'A small tithe is enough, he said, this tempter, the devil incarnate. God is easily satisfied. The path to heaven is easy. Pay ten percent and be done with it. But God will not be bribed.' "

Ruland began describing the joys of heaven. His tone was hypnotic and relaxing, the words unimportant. Traveler's eyelids drooped. His head started to tilt forward. He caught himself, glanced around to see if anyone had caught him nodding off, and realized that the women looked anything but drowsy. For them the sound of Ruland's voice was a stimulant. Their eyes shone as they watched him. Their expressions varied. The younger faces reflected lust, the older ones something softer, yet still possessive.

Melba's hand was sweating. Her grip tightened.

He leaned against her and whispered, "That's not *The Book of Mormon*."

"Has he sent you to test me?" she asked.

"Maybe," Traveler answered.

"Those are the words of God as given directly to Brother Ruland."

She took her eyes from the screen to smile at Traveler. As she did so, her eyes glittered. She licked her lips and took a deep breath, expanding her bosom. She was doing her best to look provocative.

"He told me to have faith. He told me to shed my worldly possessions in tithe. Then, and only then, would I find a celestial partner. I didn't expect anyone so young, so . . ." She looked him up and down. Her fingers writhed in his.

On screen Ruland said, "He is a false prophet. His ways are corrupt. His soul forfeit. Turn away from the false one, I beg you. His words are sharp as sin. He is deaf to all but the evil one, whose lies possess him fully."

Traveler looked away from the screen and into Melba's face. She no longer had eyes for anything but him. "Will I share you with many wives?" she said.

"No."

"God has answered my prayers."

"He must be destroyed," Ruland said.

For the first time Traveler squeezed back, feeling ashamed of himself for leading her on. "I must have missed something. Who is Ruland talking about?"

"You don't have to test me anymore. I will do anything you want."

"Answer my question, then."

"He's talking about the evil one, about Brigham Young."

26

Brother Lehi was waiting next to the car.

"Did you follow me here?" Traveler asked, annoyed at himself for failing to pick up the tail.

"Little people get away with murder, don't they?"

They were standing in a parking lot adjacent to the dental office. Every space was filled. There was little room to maneuver. Floodlights kept the dusk at bay.

"How tall are you?" Lehi asked abruptly, stepping forward aggressively as if he intended to measure himself against Traveler's chest. He stopped just short and held out a hand. "I don't even come to your goddamned shoulder."

"I'm six three."

"Bullshit. I looked you up in the record books. Six four, they listed you at. Six four and two hundred and forty pounds."

"I've lost weight since then."

"I can still take you."

"Is that why you're here?" Traveler tried to ease back a pace or two to get himself a little room. One step brought him up against a station wagon.

"Where are you going?" Lehi mocked. "I won't

hurt you." He poked himself in the chest with his thumb. "It's just me. Lilliputian Lehi. Tiny Tim. Micro man. Who could be afraid of someone like me?"

Fear had nothing to do with it, Traveler decided. But caution did. Caution in the face of madness.

Lehi stepped sideways to pivot on the balls of his feet, a dancer's pirouette. Light from the flood lamps anchored to the eaves of the dental building bathed his features. His eyes were like reflectors, bouncing the light back at Traveler.

"You're the one named for an angel," Lehi said. "But I'm the one delivering the message. Brother Ruland's littlest angel."

"Make it fast. I'm expected home for dinner."

"A man your age, still living at home." Lehi's head shook accusingly. "You ought to know better than to stick your nose into other people's religion."

"Is that Jake Ruland speaking?"

"It sure as hell ain't Joe Smith."

"Good night."

Lehi answered with another pirouette. Only this time he was building momentum for attack. His foot caught Traveler in the solar plexus, knocked the air from his lungs. He collapsed on the asphalt, his mouth working uselessly. He couldn't catch his breath. But he knew the stun was momentary. A fullback's helmet had done the same thing to him many times. The sooner he calmed himself, the sooner his lungs would start working again.

"You forgot something, didn't you, asshole?" Lehi shouted. "David and Goliath. Next time I'll finish you."

183

Traveler managed to sit up. He was still gasping, still vulnerable.

Lehi knelt beside him. "Better yet, maybe I'll go after your father. They tell me the old bastard was hot stuff in his time. Shit. If I wanted to, I could take him out with one hand behind my back." Lehi chuckled. "Maybe I'll do just that. A one-handed kill. Think about it, asshole."

Traveler made a weak grab for him. Lehi laughed and danced away.

A moment later a car door slammed, an engine revved, and Lehi was gone. The little man who wasn't there.

27

Traveler parked directly across the street from The Villa. Judging from the light spilling from windows on the top floor, Reuben Dixon was at home.

"He already thinks of me as the bad guy," Traveler told his father. "So you play good guy."

"With your size, who can blame him?"

"Just remember what I told you, Dad. Size isn't everything. If you spot this guy, Lehi, don't play games. He's dangerous."

"To think a son of mine got himself sucker-punched." Martin pretended to look to the heavens for guidance.

Traveler glanced up, too. Without falling snow, the night sky seemed particularly black, like the entrance to a cave.

They crossed the street, instinctively skirting a pool of brightness beneath a street lamp, and entered The Villa's foyer. This time the front door was locked.

Traveler pointed to the intercom. "Good guys should do the talking."

"Who am I supposed to be, the Fuller Brush man?" Martin asked softly.

"There haven't been any of those for years."

Martin punched the button next to Dixon's name. Nothing happened.

He held the button down for several seconds. Finally static crackled and a distorted voice asked, "Who is it?"

"John Varney sent me."

"What's your name?"

"Martin Traveler."

"Not Moroni?"

"I'm his father."

"Go to hell."

"Tell him we're here to talk money," Traveler whispered.

Martin repeated the message.

"Shit," Dixon said. But a moment later the door buzzed open.

They rode the elevator up to the top floor. Reuben Dixon was waiting for them in the hallway, in position to retreat into his apartment if necessary. His eyes had the glitter of a drunk.

"I thought so. Father and son. I hear you're both assholes."

He went back into his apartment but left the door open for them to follow. By the time they did he was seated on the living-room floor, his back to a shallow, brick-faced fireplace, surrounded by mounds of manila folders.

"You wouldn't hit a sitting man, would you?" he asked, peering up at Traveler. Despite the question,

Dixon looked perfectly relaxed, as if he didn't give a damn if they hit him or not.

Using the edge of his shoe, Traveler cleared an area of folders. That done, he carefully lowered himself into the carpet until he was sitting cross-legged in front of Dixon. Martin pulled up a chair.

"John Varney is too late," Dixon said, "no matter what he wants to pay. It's out of my hands now."

"What is?" Traveler said.

"Murder." Dixon reached behind him into the fireplace to retrieve an ashtray. It held a dozen homemade cigarettes ready for smoking. "We have Brigham Young to thank for this," he said, gesturing with the ashtray.

"You must be his new prophet, then," Martin said sarcastically. "Rewriting the Word of Wisdom."

"Join me?" Dixon held out the ashtray.

They both waved away the offer.

"It's like this," he said, lighting up and inhaling deeply. When time came to exhale, he half turned and blew fumes into the fireplace, no doubt to keep the neighbors from smelling the smoke. "Brigham had a dream. He'd turn southern Utah into the land of Dixie, look away, look away. But cotton couldn't make it in that god-awful place. But this shit does." He waved a cigarette. "If Brigham were alive today, it would be legal tender."

Martin looked indignant. "Are you saying the church grows marijuana?"

"Not *the* church."

"But *a* church?" Traveler put in.

"You're smarter than you look."

Now was the time, Traveler thought. Marijuana was

a much better persuader than fists. "Why did the Church of Zion Reborn pull up stakes and leave, then?"

"I told him it was a mistake at the time. Never give up a money-making business."

"Who are we talking about?" Martin's voice was whispersoft, the sound of a good guy.

"Who's asking?" Dixon said, his mood shifting abruptly. "You or John Varney?"

"Does it make a difference?"

Dixon went back to his hand-rolled cigarette. His eyes had turned black, all pupil.

Traveler grabbed him by the neck, being careful not to do any damage.

"Easy," Martin said, coming out of his chair to pry his son's fingers loose. With his back to Dixon, Martin winked like the accomplice he was.

Dixon looked unconcerned, as though nothing unusual had taken place. "Brother Jacob, of course. He gave up growing pot to harvest souls."

Traveler smiled. Suddenly it was clear how Brother Jake had financed a string of dental offices in so short a time.

"Is he harvesting your cousin, too?" Traveler said.

Dixon turned away to crush out his cigarette against the inner wall of the fireplace. "There's nothing I can do if Cousin Penny wants to screw her brains out with the likes of him."

"You have such a way with words," Traveler said, clasping his hands together to keep from overacting his role.

"I'm only a cousin by marriage. So don't get me wrong." Dixon held out his hands as if to ward off a blow. "What Penny's doing is her business. John Varney won't find out about it from me. Not with his temper. Christ. He'd send the sons of Porter Rockwell to lynch me."

"I've met Varney," Martin put in. "He's a quiet man, a scholar."

"Whatever you say. But I say they're all crazy, the whole damn family. That goes for my wife, too, living downstairs in her own apartment, for Christ's sake. But she's not as gullible as Penny. Not at all. The last time that girl was here, she and Brother Jacob were arm in arm. She actually believed some of the bullshit we were throwing around."

A malicious smile twisted Dixon's lips. "The angel's trumpet will soon sound the word of God, I told her. Look to the temple. Look to Moroni. He's getting ready to blow Brigham's cover."

"We're not theologians," Martin said.

Dixon looked from one to the other. Then he shrugged. "Why the hell shouldn't I tell you? I got tired of working on salary for Brother Jake. Look around you." He spread his arms. "A man wants more than a few apartment buildings in this life. I told him the same thing. 'Your promises,' I said, 'your big plans for the future don't pay the rent now.' That's why I went to Varney, to cash in big once so I could get out of this damned business."

He picked up a handful of folders and hurled them into the fireplace, where they lay like kindling, awaiting only a match to destroy his dreams.

"But Varney said I was a fake," Dixon continued. "Me and everything I touched. I offered to negotiate, to give him bargain-basement prices considering the merchandise. But he wouldn't budge."

The man's head shook so hard it looked like a muscle spasm. "I still don't understand how he could take that kind of risk." He hesitated for a moment. "Unless he sent you here to take it away from me?"

"That's right," Traveler improvised. He grasped Dixon by both wrists. "Varney told me to beat it out of you if need be."

Dixon cringed, but his eyes managed to remain defiant. "Look around for yourself. You can have whatever you find."

Traveler squeezed until the man grimaced. "Ruland beat you to it," Dixon blurted. "He got here before you, he and a couple of his acolytes. They cleaned me out."

Traveler decided that a new approach was needed. "You're an expert on Mormon history, aren't you?"

He awaited Dixon's nod before continuing. "The Danites of old aren't ancient history, you know. They're still here with us, protectors of our prophet's heritage. Could be you're even looking at one. Elton Woolley's avenging angel."

Dixon smiled as if to say you can't pull that one on me. But his eyes gave him away. Fear surfaced, as bright and shiny as tears.

Traveler pretended to look around the apartment. "This looks okay to me," he said finally. "The perfect location for a modern-day Mountain Meadow Massacre. Only this time, we won't pretend Indians did it. We'll make it look like Brother Jacob and his boys got to you."

"Bullshit. Things like that don't happen, not in this day and age."

His protest lacked conviction, exactly what Traveler hoped for. He nodded at his father. They rose together and walked to the door without another word.

"Bastards," Dixon spat after them. "I'm not afraid of you." His tone said otherwise.

28

With the rising of the moon the night sky revealed a thin layer of clouds, high up, caught in winds that sent them racing toward the mountains like prayers toward heaven. Watching them, Traveler felt heavy and earthbound.

He and his father were sitting in the Jeep waiting to see if Dixon panicked. At nine o'clock Martin switched on the radio to catch the news. Summer temperatures were being predicted for tomorrow. Volunteers were needed to sandbag against the expected runoff from the mountains. The Great Salt Lake was rising.

Once the announcer moved on to the usual bloodletting in the Middle East, Martin switched off the radio and said, "You see what happens when God's involved. People can't help killing each other. Jews, Arabs, Mormons, whatever."

Traveler grunted, knowing his father well enough to figure more was on the way. Martin didn't disappoint him. "Look at that moon up there."

Traveler did as he was told.

"You see any stars?"

"A few here and there."

"And planets?"

"It's hard to tell the difference."

"Not to a Mormon who believes faith will raise him to Godhood in charge of his own world."

"That reminds me," Traveler interrupted. "I ought to call Will Tanner."

"No, you don't. First you tell me just what Reuben Dixon is trying to sell to the church."

"Whatever it is, he must have forged it. Otherwise, Varney would have bought it."

"Don't be too sure that Dixon's the forger he's made out to be. That man has uncovered some important documents in the past, some favorable to the church, some not. The latter usually disappear into the archives, underground, awaiting the millennium."

"Are you trying to tell me he's selling the real thing?"

"If I knew what we were talking about I'd have a better idea."

"My guess is that we're talking Brigham Young here. Something inflammatory in writing."

Martin sighed. "What you said inside is true. I've heard talk for years of latter-day Danites sworn to protect the church."

Traveler, nodding, said, "I'll find a phone and be right back. If Dixon comes out while I'm gone, follow him until he lights somewhere, then call my service."

The 7-Eleven was the only place open nearby. Traveler used the phone in the parking lot to call Tanner at home.

"I need help, Willis."

"Officially, I don't know you. I told you that before."

"It's a question of manpower," Traveler said, knowing that the church, organized the way it was into stakes and wards, could raise an army if necessary. It had done just that back in 1857 when the federal government sent in troops under the command of General Albert Johnston to root out the evils of polygamy. In response, Brigham Young raised the Nauvoo Legion, which promptly stopped the feds in their tracks. But Brigham was too smart to continue the war. He gave in, on the surface at least, while continuing to do just as he pleased.

"Salt Lake's credit dentist," Traveler proceeded, "is a religious front. He calls each of his offices a conclave, which means that you have more than a black bishop on your hands."

"I see."

"Why is it you don't sound surprised?"

"What do you intend to do with more manpower?"

"Have each of those conclaves placed under surveillance."

"Anything else?"

"I'd like to know every move Jake Ruland makes. Reuben Dixon, too, for that matter."

"A man in my position," Tanner said calmly, "a man doing his job, would already have thought of that."

29

When Traveler returned to the car his father pretended to be asleep. But the moment the door opened he said, "I spotted our friend pacing back and forth in front of one of his windows. He looked like he was talking on the phone, one of those cordless models."

Traveler slid in behind the wheel before peering up through the wiper-smudged windshield. Drapes muted the light seeping from the windows on the top floor.

"You must have X-ray eyes," he told his father.

Martin's yawn was more contrived than his snoring. "He pulled the blinds on me just before you came back."

"We might as well go home. If we haven't flushed him out by now, we never will."

"I should have played the bad guy."

Traveler was still trying to think of a comeback when a tow truck pulled up across the street, parking parallel to the cars at the curb. A rack of amber lights on top of the cab came on and began rotating slowly. When the driver stepped out, the fluctuating light distorted his face, making him look sinister one moment and benign the next.

He checked the license plate on a Mercedes, then went to work, slipping a long metal shim through a side window to jimmy open the door. The whole procedure took only a few seconds.

He popped the hood, relocked the door, and quickly set up his tool kit next to the front tire on the driver's side. After that his upper body disappeared into the engine compartment.

"Working this late," Martin said, "I hope he's got a union."

"Maybe Dixon stayed put because his car's not working?"

"If you want to wait, it's all right with me," Martin said and began to snore again. After a moment he added, "Maybe you can keep me awake by regaling me with details of your conversation with Willis Tanner."

"With him it's always what he doesn't say that's important."

"All right. Tell me what he didn't say."

Traveler thought that over for a moment. "I have the feeling Willis has been ahead of me all the way. I wouldn't be surprised if he knew about Martha Varney's death before I did."

"That means John Varney could have known, too."

Traveler closed his eyes to recall his conversation with the man. "I don't know. Would a father keep something like that from his daughter?"

"Who can figure Mormons? Or real people either for that matter."

The lights on the top floor went out.

Traveler stretched his neck muscles, then his legs. But the Jeep wasn't designed for a man his size. Both thigh muscles cramped. He vaulted out of the car to ease the strain.

His sudden appearance startled the mechanic, who stared wildly before slamming down the Mercedes' hood and lunging to his truck.

"It's okay," Traveler called after the panic-stricken man. But the truck's engine was already turning over. He accelerated away before Traveler, limping badly, could reach him.

What the hell was going on? Traveler wondered, absently massaging the backs of his thighs. The driver's face, albeit highlighted in amber, had shown more fear than a gimpy detective should account for.

Still hobbling, Traveler made it back to the Jeep just as Reuben Dixon came out of the building. Traveler ducked. If he opened the door, the overhead light would give him away. But his stealth was for nothing.

"Fuck you, Traveler," Dixon called as soon as he had the Mercedes's door open. "You're not fooling anybody."

Traveler scrambled into the Jeep, hoping the damned thing could keep up with a Mercedes. One thing in his favor was the roads, still treacherous in spots and best suited for four-wheel-drive vehicles.

He started the engine and switched on the headlights. Their glow enabled him to see Dixon's crude, one-fingered gesture of defiance, before he got into the Mercedes.

The light blinded Traveler; the explosion deafened him. Shrapnel shattered the Jeep's windshield. Martin cried out. Or maybe it was Traveler. All in a split second.

The Jeep rocked from the shock wave.

Traveler grabbed hold of his father, feeling for broken bones, blood, anything. Martin, gasping for breath, patted him back.

Somehow they'd come through without a scratch, Traveler saw, because everything was suddenly as bright as day. The Mercedes's gas tank had ruptured. Burning fuel began racing down the gutter toward the storm drain.

"Go inside," he told his father. "Mrs. Dixon is in apartment three. Call the fire department and police."

Without waiting for an answer Traveler jumped from the Jeep and ran to the Mercedes. Luck was with him. There was no fire around the driver's seat. No door either. Just Reuben Dixon's mutilated body.

Splinters of glass and steel had been driven into his chest and belly. One hand was gone. Blood was squirting everywhere. Stemming the flow was impossible.

"Help me!" Traveler shouted. "Tell me who did it?"

Dixon's mangled lips parted. Blood immediately bubbled out of his mouth. But no sound.

"You're dying."

Dixon's tongue slid forward. For a horrifying instant Traveler thought the man was spitting it all the way out of his mouth. Then came the first words. "Tell Penny . . . I've fixed it."

"What?"

"The angel. He's ready . . ."

"Quick, man."

Dixon's final words were like a sigh. ". . . to sound the word of God."

30

The burning Mercedes attracted the moths of night, a motorcyclist from the 7-Eleven down the street, a customized Chevy riding high on oversize tires, gawkers from the neighboring apartments, disheveled by sleep but as bright-eyed as vampires.

The sound of approaching sirens, running up and down the scale like mechanical coyotes, sent Traveler inside. His father opened the door to apartment three. Behind him stood Mrs. Dixon, her face tight with grief.

"I have to go to Reuben," she said, making a lunge toward the door.

Traveler blocked her way with his shoulder. Two days ago she'd possessed that fragile beauty some women achieve in middle age. Now she looked as old as Traveler felt.

"Maybe he's not dead," she said, clawing at his arm. "Maybe it's a mistake."

He looked to his father for guidance. Martin only shook his head.

"The police are just arriving," Traveler told her. "Leave it to them."

She struck at him, but her fists were ineffectual against his heavy clothing. Her fists opened, became claws aimed at his face.

Martin caught her from behind. She struggled wildly for a moment, then went limp. Martin didn't let go until she started crying.

"Please let me see him," she managed to say after a moment. "I have to talk to him. We had a fight this afternoon. I told him I hated him. I didn't mean it. I don't want those to be the last words he heard."

"Words aren't important," Martin said softly. "He knows you loved him."

"Did I?" She looked at Martin in surprise. "Yes. I guess I did."

"It might help to tell somebody," Traveler said, trying to pry tactfully.

". . . About your fight," Martin said, picking up quickly on his son's intentions.

She looked stunned, staring at first one man and then the other.

"The police will be here soon," Traveler said. "After that, nothing you say can be confidential." He winced at the implication of his words. He was deliberately misleading her, offering her the sanctity of the confessional without any guarantee of privacy.

Sounds from outside intruded: another siren, a distant dog howling accompaniment, the screech of metal against concrete.

Mrs. Dixon backed away from the men until she found herself against the sofa. She collapsed into it, sagging against the cushions. Her head tilted back until she was staring at the ceiling.

Traveler was about to speak again when she suddenly struggled to her feet and exchanged the sofa for her rocking chair. Once seated again, she looked down at her lap. "The last day or so my husband acted crazy. One minute we were talking here in my apartment, the next he dragged me up to the roof. 'I want you to take one last look,' he said and pointed me toward the temple. It was snowing. You could just see the Angel Moroni. 'I'm bringing him down,' Reuben shouted. 'Who?' I said. 'God?' 'Him, too,' he answered. 'He and that angel of His.' "

She paused, gasping for breath, her head angled toward the wall to avoid their eyes. "I struggled but he wouldn't let go of me. 'Oh, no, you don't,' he said. 'You have to hear this. I want you to know who's responsible. I came up with the idea, not that dentist. He thinks he's going to use it. But I'm the brains.' "

Mrs. Dixon's head snapped around to face Traveler. Her cheeks were wet with tears. "I still love him. That's my sin."

"What do you know about Jake Ruland?" Traveler asked.

"That man procured women for my husband, I'm sure of it. He's evil. I feel it every time he's near me. He turned my husband against the church. It wasn't Reuben talking when he said he'd bring down God. It was that man Ruland."

"What did your husband mean?"

"I don't know. He wouldn't say. He wouldn't listen to me either when I begged him to reaffirm his faith." Sobs wracked her body until she was bending at the waist in an effort to catch her breath.

Lieutenant Anson Horne arrived on the scene before she had time to recover. He took one look at Traveler and his father and had them escorted outside.

Floodlights illuminated the front of the apartment building, giving it the look of an overexposed snapshot. Investigators and gawkers had trampled the entire area into a quagmire.

Their escort, two uniformed officers, marched them all the way to the Jeep.

"Is there anything keeping us from going home?" Traveler asked as he opened the door.

"The lieutenant has your car keys," one of the cops said.

"Perfect," Martin said and began scraping the soles of his galoshes against what passed for a running board.

The sight of his father at work started Traveler thinking. More adrenaline kicked in, stimulating his memory. He recalled his first trip to the Varney house, in particular the kitchen. There, atop newspapers spread over the tile floor, stood Pearl Varney's galoshes. They were muddy, too. Only not with plain old Salt Lake sludge, but the blood-colored soil of southern Utah.

31

Traveler and his father were questioned twice by Lieutenant Horne and once by an assistant from the District Attorney's office before being sent home. Neither interrogator seemed satisfied with Traveler's explanation as to how he and Martin happened to be in the right place to witness a murder.

As they pulled into their own driveway a few minutes before midnight his father said, " 'Behold, the devil hath deceived me; for he appeared unto me in the form of an angel, and said unto me: Go and reclaim this people, for they have all gone astray after an unknown God. And he said unto me: There is no God.' "

"You're not going religious on me, are you?"

"Why not? I'm getting old, too old for this kind of thing. I told you before, if you work for the church you have to play by their rules. And their rules change to fit the occasion, even for murder."

"I didn't know you could quote from *The Book of Mormon*," Traveler said to avoid an argument, theological or otherwise.

"My mother used to read the damned stuff to me

every night. That's the trouble when you get old. You can remember the past fine, but not what happened yesterday." He opened the car door and started to get out.

"I'm not coming in," Traveler said.

Martin's body froze in place, while his head came around to face his son. The overhead light cast shadows dark enough to turn his eyes into black holes. "Where the hell are you going this time of night?"

Traveler decided against mentioning Pearl Varney's galoshes.

"Okay," Martin said, gesturing surrender with his hands, "but you're coming inside for a cup of coffee first. I don't want you falling asleep at the wheel."

Traveler grumbled but got out of the Jeep.

A manila envelope was taped to the front door. A single word, Moroni, was scrawled across it. Traveler recognized Claire's handwriting.

So did his father. "That's all you needed," he said, pulling the envelope loose before opening the door. Once inside, he handed it to Traveler and then disappeared into the kitchen.

For a moment Traveler considered leaving the envelope unopened. Morning, the rational light of day, would be soon enough to deal with Claire. Better yet, ignore it altogether. But he knew that was impossible. Curiosity and old lust wouldn't allow it.

"Do you want anything in your coffee?" Martin called out.

Traveler was tempted. Something alcoholic to dull the edge of memory.

"Black and strong," he shouted back.

"Ten minutes," Martin answered, his way of being

204

diplomatic, of telling his son just how much time he had alone to himself.

The envelope contained a letter and half a dozen Polaroid photographs.

> *Dear Moroni,*
> *I know how you love playing detective, so I thought we could play together. Six clues are enclosed. Work them out correctly and you'll be able to find me in no time at all. If you do, I'll love you as never before. If you don't, I'll know you no longer care.*
> *Love,*
> *Claire.*
> *P.S.—For help with the clues you can reach me at one of the numbers on the backs of the Polaroids.*

One after the other he turned over the snapshots. Each one had a different telephone number. As for the pictures, they were all of Claire, looming large in the foreground while the backgrounds were undoubtedly meant as clues. He identified a bar, a gas station, a cemetery, and a Mormon church, distinguishable because of its utilitarian architecture. (When it came to their churches, Mormons were strictly pragmatists. No-frills religion. Even the main meeting rooms were convertible, so they could be used as basketball floors to promote youth leagues.) The backgrounds in the other two photos were less obvious.

He decided that phoning six telephone numbers would be easier than trying to read the machinations of Claire's mind into each of the Polaroids. But midnight was not the best time to call. Or do anything else for that matter.

"Forget the coffee," he told his father. "I'm going to lie down for a while."

The first telephone number that Traveler tried in the morning was the Holy Cross Hospital, the second the city morgue. Claire was playing more than detective. She was making him relive his first frantic search for her, when he'd suspected the worst.

She answered on his third try. "I've been waiting all night," she complained.

"I'm on a case."

"You've been with another woman?" It was half question, half accusation.

"Sure."

"You don't deserve my help with the clues."

"I know." Listening to Claire's voice brought her image back to him so vividly. Beautiful but bone-thin when they first met, with almost no breasts to speak of. But as soon as they began living together she had started gaining weight, though without ever seeming to eat. Her voice, now that he thought about it, sounded hungry, as if he were what she fed upon.

"Why did you call, then?"

"To hear the sound of your voice."

"What's wrong, Moroni? Are you sick?"

"Just tired, that's all." Even talking to her was draining him of energy.

There was a moment's hesitation before she said, "Well, you have to find me today, then. Otherwise, the game's over."

"Fine."

"Does that mean you're not going to play?"

Traveler closed his eyes. "For once we're going to use my rules."

"What?"

"You find me."

"But I know where you are."

"No, Claire. That's one thing you've never known."

32

The sun was shining in Federal Heights. Spring
lawns, not yet fully green, were emerging from beneath the melting snow. Runoff had the gutters over-
flowing. A rooster-tail of spray kicked up where the
rushing waters pounded against the tires of Will Tanner's car, which was parked at the curb in front of the
Varney house.

It was Tanner who opened the door. He was smiling,
his face relaxed. His squint was gone.

"Somehow I expected you to show up on our door-
step this morning." His voice was as cheerful as the
sunshine but did nothing to enlighten Traveler.

"Why are you here, Willis?"

"I go where I'm needed. This is a difficult time for
the Varneys. No matter what kind of man Dixon was,
he was still part of their family." Tanner's smile persisted. "His widow stayed the night here. John and
Pearl were a great comfort to her."

Traveler looked closely at his friend. Sunlight reflected through the crystals of the chandelier, casting
abstract patterns on his face, turning his smile jagged
as though cut into a Halloween pumpkin.

"I'm glad you've come, Mo. The prophet wanted me to thank you personally for your help last night. The police department will be commending you, too, in writing. You're a hero. There's a distinct possibility of a bonus." His tone of voice was bright enough to make Traveler suspicious.

"I'm being rude, aren't I? Keeping you standing here in the doorway. There's hot cocoa on the stove in the kitchen."

Tanner led the way. While pouring the cocoa with one hand he gestured enthusiastically with the other. "It was your tip that did it, Mo. Because of it, we staked out every one of Jake Ruland's offices."

"Hold on. When I talked to you on the phone last night I got the impression that you already knew about him."

"Elton Woolley is smiling on you. Do you know what that means in this town? And you a gentile."

"I like you better when you're sweating, Willis."

Tanner, who was leaning against the kitchen counter in front of the sink, tested the cocoa and theatrically smacked his lips. "Even as we speak, one of Jake Ruland's assistants is being arrested for the murder of Reuben Dixon. Our lookouts spotted him driving a tow truck. That, combined with your eyewitness account of what happened, will put him away for murder. Besides which, we have his army records. They taught him demolition before dentistry. We feel certain that he'll implicate Ruland as an accomplice. The fact is, I have Anson Horne's guarantee on that."

"And if he can't deliver?"

Tanner peered into his cup and made a face. "What am I thinking about? There's caffeine in this stuff." A tic pulled at the skin around one eye, the forerunner of a squint.

"Why is it I don't trust you, Willis?"

Tanner turned around to dump the remains of his cocoa into the sink. When he faced Traveler again, his squint had come back. "You got here too early, Mo. I haven't had time to deliver the rest of the bad news to John Varney."

Traveler had come with the intention of bestowing some bad news of his own but hadn't counted on Tanner as a witness.

"Just how bad is it?"

Tanner chewed at his lip. "For a man like him? The worst, probably."

"You'll need my moral support, then."

"I can't do that. This is church business. Strictly confidential."

"Consider my presence the bonus you were talking about."

Tanner drew a deep breath, letting it out in a long sigh. "I'll have to make a call first."

Traveler pointed to a wall phone at the end of the tile counter.

Tanner's sigh turned into a groan of resignation. He stepped to the phone, using his body to shield the buttons from Traveler, and punched in the number. Almost immediately he said, "There's a complication, sir. Moroni Traveler is here. He insists on being present during my interview with Brother Varney."

Tanner stopped speaking and began to nod. After a few moments he said, "Yes, sir. I'll remind him."

Following a few more *Yes, sirs,* he hung up the phone and reported, "The prophet trusts you, Mo.

But he wants me to remind you that client privacy is involved here. Whatever you hear goes no further."

"Am I officially on the payroll, then?"

"For all intents and purposes."

Which meant Traveler would be expendable should push come to shove.

"When I saw you coming up the walk a few minutes ago, I told the Varneys to wait in the den until I called them," Tanner said, sounding somewhat awed by the authority conferred upon him. "We'll see them now."

They found John Varney seated at his antique partners' desk, his back to his leather-bound books. Pearl stood at his side, one hand resting on his shoulder. They reminded Traveler of one of those posed photographs touched up to look like an oil painting.

Tanner slid into the facing chair, pushing the telephone to one side so that nothing was between them. Traveler remained in the background, leaning against the study's heavy oak door.

"What's he doing here?" Varney asked immediately, nodding at Traveler.

"The prophet wants it that way," Tanner said.

Varney's mouth fell open. His jaw worked up and down but no sound came out. Finally he looked up at his sister, whose hand was massaging his shoulder reassuringly. He forced a smile. His teeth snapped down on whatever complaint he'd been about to utter.

Tanner, speaking softly, recounted the facts of Dixon's murder. He had dropped to a near-whisper by the time he reached his conclusion. "Everything points to a conspiracy led by Jake Ruland."

"Why do you sound surprised?" Varney countered. "We all know he's a black bishop."

"I'm sorry," Tanner said after a moment's hesitation. "Your daughter has become one of his wives."

"That's a lie."

Pearl closed her eyes, though not before tears escaped. "Where were they married?" she asked.

Varney snapped, "There was no marriage."

"Certainly not in the temple," Tanner went on as if unopposed. "The fact is, Penny's excommunication will be considered when the apostles meet tomorrow."

Pearl Varney's hands went to her mouth but were unable to stifle her agonized sobbing.

"I demand a chance to speak before the apostles," Varney said.

"I have nothing to say about that. I'm only the messenger."

Varney's fists pounded the green leather desktop hard enough to dislodge the phone. "Dammit," he muttered, snatching the instrument from the floor. "I'll call the prophet myself." He punched the buttons violently. Veins stood out on his neck. His entire body shook with the effort of self-control as he pressed the receiver against his ear. He looked like a man about to explode.

Pearl's sobs stopped as she held her breath.

The room was quiet enough for Traveler to hear the phone ringing at the other end. The sound went on and on.

"Your number is no longer in use," Tanner said. "A decision on future access has yet to be reached."

Varney glared across the desk, his eyes wide like those of a cornered animal. The phone in his hand came away from his ear and suddenly looked like a weapon.

Traveler eased away from the door and into position to protect Tanner if necessary.

Then all at once the fire in Varney died. His eyes glazed. He stood up slowly, like a man in a trance. "The prophet will see me if I go to him in person. If I beg." He walked out of the room without another word.

"They won't let him anywhere near Woolley," Tanner said. "He must know that. He knows procedure."

"Maybe you ought to go after him, Willis."

"If he wants to waste his time, it's nothing to me."

From the side of the house came the sound of a car engine starting up.

"He could cause a fuss, maybe even generate some bad publicity."

The car drove away.

"My God. I never thought of that." Tanner ran from the room. The front door slammed, followed a few seconds later by the sound of another revving engine.

Through it all Pearl Varney hadn't moved, but remained standing at attention like a soldier awaiting orders. Traveler took her by the shoulders and guided her into her brother's vacant chair.

Then he knelt down beside her. "Why didn't you tell Penny that her mother was dead?"

She stared at him, unblinking. But her eyes were alive and defiant.

"You're forgetting something," he said. "I saw your galoshes in the kitchen that first day I came here. They were covered with red mud, the kind you pick up in southern Utah."

Her head turned slowly from side to side denying any such allegation.

"There's an old man living in Hurricane. He told me a woman had been there ahead of me to see Martha Varney's grave. If I showed him your photograph, I'm quite certain he could identify you."

"What does it matter? There's nothing left of my family. You and that man, Tanner, have seen to that. You've destroyed everything, all my years of work to save us gone for nothing."

She hugged herself, at the same time sighing so hard she seemed to shrink. "Why do you suppose I went looking for Martha in the first place?" she asked, gesturing away any need for a response. "I thought that if I found her, if I proved to Penny that her mother was still alive, why then everything would be all right again. I thought Penny would come back to us, be our little girl again. But when I discovered that Martha was dead, I couldn't tell Penny such a thing, though Martha had gotten exactly what was coming to her. Her own adultery killed her, Mr. Traveler. That man she was living with, in sin, beat her to death. It was a judgment."

She stopped speaking and stared at him. Her expression seemed to want acknowledgment from him, agreement that God and justice were on her side. He said nothing.

She nodded as if affirming some preconceived notion of her own. "Good riddance, I say, Mr. Traveler. I thought my brother would feel the same way. But I should have guessed. Men are so weak. Even after all those years, after all Martha had done, he still loved her."

"Did you tell him about Earl Jordan?"

"What else could I do? My brother went there to

inflict a beating on the man, nothing more. A little justice, not God's vengeance. The shooting was an accident.''

''The police don't believe in accidents when they're reported this long after the fact.''

''I'm not reporting it. If you do, I'll confess myself. You'll never prove otherwise.''

33

Traveler dialed an emergency telephone number that Will Tanner had given him a long time ago, one guaranteed to work no matter what. An operator answered after the first ring. Her voice sounded incredulous, as though no one had ever called her before. If the church was running true to form, she was probably speaking from one of the lower, bombproof levels of the LDS office building.

"I wish to speak to Willis Tanner," Traveler told her. "Immediately."

"Your authorization code, please."

He thought about saying "life or death," but settled for, "I'm a detective and this is an emergency."

She hesitated. "You should have been provided with a code."

"I'm sorry."

"Name?"

As Traveler provided the information he could hear the sound of keys typing in data to a computer. No doubt *lost soul* was flashing on her screen right now. Or worse.

"I'll have to put you on hold," she said, doing just that without waiting for a response.

No Mormon Tabernacle Choir this time, only Mountain Bell's static.

Traveler rubbed his eyes hard enough to produce a kaleidoscope of bursting images. When they faded he saw in his mind's eye a montage of faces, all distorted by the self-inflicted pain of religious flagellation. Three people were dead: Earl Jordan, Martha Varney, and Reuben Dixon. One way or another Utah's God had a hand in their killing. And there was more violence to come, he felt certain of it.

The line cleared. "Mo, is that you?" Tanner asked, his voice a deferential whisper.

"Did you get to Varney?"

"No, I lost him."

"Where?"

"He turned off South Temple before he got downtown. He must have changed his mind about seeing the prophet, otherwise he would have kept straight on. But I didn't take any chances. I came right here to the Hotel Utah. There's no sign of his car. President Woolley hasn't been disturbed, thank God."

"Call the police. I think Varney has another target in mind."

"Target?" Tanner said, his voice rising.

"He killed Earl Jordan. My guess is he intends to do the same thing to Jake Ruland."

"What the hell are you talking about?" Tanner said, no longer making any attempt to whisper.

"I told you before. There's a rumor, probably true, that Jordan beat his common-law wife, Martha Varney, to death. What you didn't know, and neither did

I until just a few minutes ago, is that John Varney never stopped loving her. His motive was simple revenge. Ruland's participation in Martha's death wasn't all that certain. But when you add Penny and excommunication into the equation, I think Varney is about to kill again. He's an old-fashioned man. He believes in blood atonement.''

Enough silence followed to make Traveler ask, ''Are you still there, Willis?''

''It's all right. Leave everything to me.''

34

The blowup of Dr. Jake stood out front of the dentist's Main Street office. Traveler pulled into a parking place next to an out-of-state car with Missouri license plates that proclaimed it the "show me" state. The sight of it brought a grim smile to his face. His grandfather on his mother's side, a fanatic LDSer, had always referred to Missourians as "pukes," a nickname they'd earned by driving Mormons out of their state back in the 1830s.

Traveler got out of the Jeep and started toward the door. Suddenly he stopped and looked up and down the street. Where were the police cars? There had been plenty of time, fifteen minutes at least, for Will Tanner to alert them. The light, midmorning traffic wouldn't have been any problem.

Christ, he thought, patting his shoulder holster for reassurance. Up the street Brigham Young's statue still had its back to the temple. Traveler would have liked something just as solid behind him.

With a shake of his head, he passed by the cardboard mockup and went inside. Penny was at her desk as usual, although her receptionist's smile had been replaced by tears.

"What's happened?" he asked.

"Daddy burst in here a few minutes ago. He was acting crazy. He called me names."

Traveler looked around. No one was in the waiting area.

"I sent them home," Penny explained through a sob.

"Where's your father now?"

"Inside with Dr. Jake."

"And Lehi?"

"He went out on an errand a little while ago."

"I'm going inside. Call the police. If Lehi gets here before they do, warn me."

He drew his .45 and crept down the carpeted hallway that led to Dr. Jake's office. Even so, John Varney heard him coming.

"I'm not afraid of dying," he called out before Traveler reached the open door.

"That puts you one up on me."

"I know that's you, Mr. Traveler. I'm armed."

Traveler flattened himself against the wall.

"I'm doing God's work."

"How do you know?"

"I won't debate with you, Mr. Traveler. Put your gun on the carpet and slide it in here."

Better to retreat, Traveler thought, than to put himself in Varney's hands.

"Do what he says," Dr. Jake said, his voice brittle with fear. "Please."

"He's become very talkative for a dentist," Varney said. "You might learn something."

Shit, Traveler thought and knelt down. He set the gun on safety and eased it around the doorjamb.

"That's fine. You can come in now."

Traveler peeked around the corner. Varney had one foot on the .45. Next to him sat Dr. Jake. Cloth bibs had been used to tie his hands and feet to the dental chair.

"I want you there against the wall by the window," Varney said, gesturing with his own revolver. "Sit on your hands if you don't mind."

Walking on his knees, Traveler crossed over to the location indicated and sat, his back to the window. He was facing a terrified-looking Jake Ruland.

Varney slowly backed up, carefully reaching behind to find the dentist's work stool. Once seated on that, he jammed the revolver's barrel into Dr. Jake's ear and cocked the hammer. Throughout the maneuver he'd kept the .45 underfoot.

Varney sighed and said, "I'm going to pull the trigger sooner or later, Mr. Traveler. If you make any sudden moves it will be a lot sooner."

Dr. Jake's eyes rolled as he tried to get a look at Varney without moving his head. "For God's sake," the dentist pleaded. "Can't you do something to help me?"

Varney's lips curled in contempt. "If you're God's prophet as you claim to be, He'll hear you and smite me down." Varney looked up as if awaiting judgment. But his gun didn't waver. "Well, I'm waiting."

"Please," the dentist said to Traveler. "You can't let him kill me."

"Give me a reason."

The dentist's jaw dropped open. "I—"

"You can start by telling me what happened at Blood Butte."

"Confession is for Catholics," Varney interrupted. "This man has destroyed the love in my life. First Martha and now my daughter."

Where the hell are the police? Traveler wondered.

"Martha killed herself, just like I said," Dr. Jake blurted out. "She climbed the butte and jumped off."

"Liar," Varney shouted, jabbing the gun barrel hard enough to draw blood.

Dr. Jake squealed. "I only wanted to protect my people. What else could I do? Earl Jordan came to me and confessed. He'd gotten drunk and hit Martha. He didn't know his own strength. Her neck broke."

"That's not good enough. Earl was one of your apostles."

"A false apostle. God punished him."

"No. I did that. That's how I know you're lying."

Fear widened the dentist's eyes.

"Earl got down on his knees to me," Varney said.

"I'll do it, too," the dentist cried.

"I put the gun in his mouth and told him to pray. After that, he told me everything. How you and he started drinking together after he killed her. How the two of you decided to make it look like an accident. I knew then that I would get even with you someday, somehow."

In the silence that followed Traveler heard a noise in the hall.

"Please, Father," Penny said. She sounded very close. "Let him go." There was more fear than plea in her voice.

"Did you call the police?" Traveler called to her.

222

"I . . ." Penny began, then cried out in pain.

"Tell him, honey," a soft voice said.

"Lehi," Dr. Jake breathed as if his prayers had been answered. "My true disciple."

"Go on, honey," Lehi said. "Convince him before I do some real damage."

"I didn't want the police to arrest my father," Penny blurted. "I . . . I'm sorry."

"Give it up in there," Lehi said, "or I'm going to kill her."

"She's already dead," Varney answered. " 'And I say unto you again that he cannot save them in their sins; for I cannot deny his word, and he hath said that no unclean thing can inherit the kingdom of heaven.' "

Penny screamed.

Moving his foot slowly, Varney began edging the .45 in Traveler's direction.

"Hey, Varney," Lehi said, "you ever screwed a woman standing up?"

Cloth ripped.

"Daddy," Penny cried.

"Throw out your gun or I'll give it to her right here."

In desperation, Varney kicked the .45. Traveler scooped it up and snapped off the safety.

"If that's the way you want it," Lehi said.

Penny groaned.

"My cock belongs on a seven-footer," Lehi bragged.

Varney, his revolver pressing into the dentist's ear, looked straight at Traveler and mouthed, "Save my daughter." Then he pulled the trigger. A piece of Jake Ruland's head exploded through the window that looked out on Main Street. The man must have died instantly, though his spasming body didn't seem to know it.

Despite the ringing in his ears Traveler heard a loud thump outside the door, followed by the sound of retreating footsteps. He crawled to the doorway, angling himself so that he could see some of the corridor without fully exposing himself. Penny lay crumpled against the far wall, her eyes dazed. Blood trickled from her mouth where Lehi had hit her.

Traveler clenched his teeth in frustration and began picking his way along the hallway. When he reached the reception area it was empty. The front door stood wide open.

He called the police.

35

John Varney was sitting on the floor, cradling his daughter in his arms and softly singing a lullaby, when the first police units arrived. Will Tanner wasn't far behind. Lieutenant Horne was with him.

"What the hell kept you?" Traveler asked.

Horne ignored the question and demanded to know what happened. As soon as Traveler told him, two uniformed policemen jerked Varney roughly to his feet and handcuffed him. While that was happening Penny kept reaching out to her father.

Traveler took her by the arms and gently raised her from the floor. Once standing she leaned against him for support. Her vacant eyes stared straight ahead.

"I don't want you talking," Tanner told Varney. "Not to anyone but our lawyer."

As one of the chosen, a member of the Council of Seventy, Varney was assured of special treatment. At the moment, however, his only response was a perfunctory nod.

"You heard the man," Horne said to the officers flanking Varney. "Take him to the jail. Don't say a word to him on the way. Pass that order along to the booking sergeant."

They nodded and led Varney down the hall, handling him much more gingerly than before.

Traveler slipped one arm around Penny's waist to prop her up. His free hand tapped Tanner on the shoulder. "Did you call the police when I asked you to?"

Horne's double take rivaled a silent movie actor's. "Is there something I don't know?"

Tanner raised a hand, motioning for silence. "I am speaking for the prophet now. For you to persist in questioning me at this time would be . . . unfortunate."

"Damn you," Traveler said. "You could have prevented this."

"It's better this way," Tanner responded quietly. "Now we can round up Brother Ruland's flock and bring them back into the fold."

Penny's limp body jerked to attention. "What does he mean, Mr. Traveler?" Shock was wearing away, being replaced by anger.

"I'm not sure," Traveler said, though he had some nasty suspicions. It was quite possible that Tanner had waited deliberately, hoping for exactly what happened, the timely removal of Jake Ruland. On second thought, however, that didn't seem logical. Wouldn't the church be better off with Jake Ruland alive, and facing charges in the death of Reuben Dixon, than to have a member of the Council of Seventy stand trial for murder? Or maybe Tanner was praying for a quiet suicide to tie up all the loose ends. Traveler shook his head at the thought. A man with John Varney's convictions wouldn't go to meet God with that kind of sin on his conscience. Unless, of course, someone helped him along by pulling the trigger for him.

Traveler said, "There's only one thing I know for sure, Penny. Your father is a sick man."

Tanner jumped in. "He'll be out on bail in a few hours. You have my word on it."

"Are you speaking for the prophet now?" she asked.

"For all intents and purposes I am."

Penny stepped away from Traveler. Lehi's blow had left her lips puffy. She spoke without moving them. "Fine. You tell him for me then that I blame him for everything that's happened. Him and the church. There's no escape from it in this damned city. It sent my mother fleeing to her death, and now my father has to pay."

She looked up at Traveler. "I should have known better than to ask you for help. No good can come from anyone named for that angel."

Traveler took her by the elbow. "I'll drive you home."

She pulled out of his grasp. "I'm going to the jail to look after my father."

"I'll take you there, then."

She glared first at Traveler, then Tanner. "All right," she said finally. "I guess you're the lesser of two evils."

Traveler didn't speak again until they were driving toward the center of town. "Reuben Dixon told me something before he died. It was a message for you."

The lanes ahead were empty of traffic, so he took his eyes from the road long enough to check her reaction to such a revelation. But she remained inert, slumped against the passenger door, her cheek resting on the window.

"It was something about angels."

Out of the corner of his eye he saw her shift position until she was staring at him.

"Dixon wanted you to know that he fixed it so the angel of God is ready to sound the word. Do you know what he meant?"

Her laughter was brief. "I win after all. He's given me a way to bring down God."

"I see," he said, though he didn't.

His tone must have sounded condescending, because she immediately responded, "I don't care if you believe me or not. Brigham Young is coming down."

"I thought you said God was."

"Around here it amounts to the same thing."

The police building was just ahead. He pulled into the lot and took the first available parking place.

"The funny thing is," Penny continued, "Reuben was always careful to remain a member of the church in good standing. That way he had access to original scripture and the like. That's how he knew Brigham Young's handwriting when he saw it."

"What are you talking about?"

"I overheard him explaining it to Dr. Jake. He had something in writing that would prove that Brigham Young was a murderer."

"It must have been a forgery."

"I don't know. Dr. Jake didn't seem to think so."

Traveler thought he knew what was coming but asked the question anyway. "Who's he supposed to have murdered?"

"Joe Smith, of course. That's how he got control of the church. That's—"

"I've heard that one before," Traveler interrupted. "It's one of those rumors that never seem to die."

"The truth survives," Penny said stubbornly.

"Not without a little help from Reuben Dixon."

"That's right. He told me once that he didn't really trust Jake Ruland to use the document properly. In an emergency, he said, he'd stash it inside Moroni's trumpet. So all you have to do now is drop me off in front of the temple and I'll go get it."

He started the engine. "Does anybody else know about the hiding place?"

"Dr. Jake probably did. It was his suggestion originally."

"I thought you said Dixon didn't trust him."

"That's the beauty of it. As a black bishop Dr. Jake would have never been allowed anywhere near Moroni without an escort."

"And Lehi?"

"My God. I forgot about him. Dr. Jake always said he had no secrets from Brother Lehi. But don't worry. They won't let him in the temple. He's not a member in good standing."

Instead of heading for the temple, Traveler turned north toward Federal Heights. "I'm taking you home."

"I won't stay there."

He didn't argue; he just kept driving. When he reached the Varney house he took her by the wrist and dragged her to the door.

Pearl Varney opened up before he had time to

knock. "The police just called," she said. "My brother has been arrested. I was about to go to him."

"We know," Traveler said.

"It can't be true."

"But it is," Penny blurted and threw herself into her aunt's arms.

"There, there," Pearl said, stroking Penny's head.

"Listen to me," Traveler said. "If you love Penny, keep her here. Don't let her out of your sight for the next few hours."

"I'll do no such thing," the woman said. "Our place is with John."

"Dammit. She's already been attacked once."

In the face of Traveler's anger, Pearl Varney backed up a step, dragging her niece along with her. Her hands went to Penny's bruised lips. "Who did this?"

"A maniac named Lehi," Traveler said. "He would have raped Penny if your brother hadn't killed Jake Ruland first."

"Dear God."

"Now will you do as I say?"

Her eyes went wide. Her mouth opened as if she intended to say something, but all she could manage was a nod.

36

Rather than waste time looking for a public telephone, Traveler drove directly home. He broke the speed limit all the way.

His father was still in his bathrobe. When Martin opened his mouth to offer greetings, Traveler charged right on by to the phone. He dialed Tanner's emergency number. This time the operator gave him no hassle; she patched him through to Tanner's present location, the police department.

"I have to see you, Willis."

"I'm waiting for a judge."

"This is more important."

"What are you talking about?"

"Meet me at the temple. Better yet, make it my office."

"What's happened?"

"A problem's come up. It's not something the church would want talked about over the phone."

"How soon?"

"Ten minutes."

The moment Traveler hung up, his father, who'd

crept into the hall to eavesdrop, said, "I'm coming with you."

"You're damn right. This is one time I want someone covering my back."

Willis Tanner was waiting for them in front of the Chester Building, huddled in the doorway, his neck scrunched into the collar of a heavy overcoat. There was still enough snow on the ground to add bite to the breeze blowing off the lake. The sky had clouded over once again.

"It's about time," he said. "I'm freezing."

"It will be hot enough when you arrive in hell," Traveler said.

"That's not funny."

"Jake Ruland's not laughing either."

"I didn't come here to argue."

"Why didn't you wait for me inside?"

"It smells like cigar smoke in there."

"Come on," Traveler said, leading the way.

The elevator operator, Nephi Bates, gave Tanner a knowing look before taking them to the top. Traveler's office was hot and stuffy, the result of air rising from the floors below. Yet Tanner didn't remove his coat. It was his way of saying that he wasn't planning to stay long.

"We've got a problem," Traveler said as soon as he closed the door. "Reuben Dixon was sharper than any of us thought. He had something worth killing for, so he took out his own nasty kind of insurance."

"Am I supposed to know what you're talking about?" Tanner said.

"Don't take it personally," Martin put in. "I don't know what's going on either."

"He had a document," Traveler continued, "supposedly in Brigham Young's handwriting—"

"Wait a minute," Tanner broke in. "Have you seen this so-called document yourself?"

"I'm just reporting what I heard."

Tanner sat heavily on the edge of the desk. His sigh sounded suspiciously like one of relief. "Keep going."

"It's supposed to prove that Brigham Young was behind the killing of Joseph Smith."

Tanner smiled, looking definitely relieved. "That's old news. I've heard that story a hundred times."

"You're not out of the woods yet, Willis. Dixon hid the damned thing in the temple."

"What?" Tanner launched himself from the desktop.

"I don't know if it's a forgery or not. But finding it in the temple would be one way of giving it provenance."

"Shit!"

"There's more. I may not be the only one who knows where it is."

Tanner leaned forward. "All right, Mo. How much do you want?"

Traveler grabbed the front of Tanner's overcoat and slammed him against the desk. "You son of a bitch. You have the gall to say that to me." He shook Tanner until his head flopped back and forth. "A man's dead because of you."

Without warning Traveler released him and stepped back. "Go ahead, take a poke at me, Willis. Give me an excuse to defend myself."

Tanner blinked repeatedly. His lips trembled. But

there was no sign of fear, only anguish. "Don't you think I know what I've done?" He looked down at his hands as if expecting to see blood.

"Then why didn't you call the police?"

"I do God's work."

Traveler glared.

"Please, Mo. I've got to know where that document is. I'm begging you."

"All right. Take me with you. I'd like to be there when you find it."

"In the temple?"

Traveler nodded.

"You're a gentile, for God's sake. I can't let you on sacred ground. I . . ." He paused, his squint more distorted than ever. "Mo, you're my friend but . . ."

Tanner's beeper went off before Traveler had time to finish his thought.

"That has to be Elton Woolley," he said, snatching up the phone and dialing quickly. Almost immediately he said, "It's me, sir. Will Tanner."

Martin made a face, somewhere between awe and anger.

"My God," Tanner said. "I'll be right there."

When he hung up and turned to face Traveler again, tears were in his eyes. "It's too late. Someone's beaten us to it. They broke into the temple. Two guards have been killed." He cast a look over his shoulder. The spires of the temple were framed in the office window behind him. "I have to go."

"The document's up there on top," Traveler said, stepping to the glass and pointing. "In Moroni's trumpet."

Tanner gripped Traveler's hand before rushing out.

37

Side by side, Traveler and his father stood at the window, staring at the temple. A shaft of sunlight slipped through an opening in the clouds and moved like a searchlight across the spires until it reached the Angel Moroni.

Traveler blinked. He rubbed his eyes. But the shadow at the base of Moroni's tower didn't go away. It moved in fact.

He retrieved the telescopic sight from among the pieces of his disassembled M1 rifle and took aim on the angel's tower.

"By God," he murmured, handing the scope to his father. "Look at that."

"Who is it?"

"Jake Ruland's disciple. His name's Lehi."

"That doesn't tell me a hell of a lot."

Traveler took back the scope and studied the spire again. Judging by Lehi's rate of progress, he still had a minute or so to go before he reached the angel. At the moment he was attempting to lasso it.

"He probably doesn't know there's a way up into Moroni from the inside," Traveler said.

"How do you know?"

"There's no other explanation if the document's really there. Reuben Dixon was no mountain climber. If Lehi gets hold of it now, he's got a hostage. The church will have to let him walk away free and clear."

"That's not your problem."

But it is, Traveler thought, as his memory replayed Lehi's threat. *I could kill your father with one hand if I wanted to.*

Traveler began assembling the rifle.

"God help us," Martin said, then began a running commentary of Lehi's progress. "He's just about there, maybe an arm's length from Moroni's feet."

The barrel slipped into its well-worn wooden stock.

"He's attaching something to the angel. It looks like a safety harness."

The trigger housing snapped into place.

"No. It's a rig to hold something else."

The scope locked into position.

"He's got an acetylene torch."

Traveler fed in the ammunition clip.

He hardly felt the recoil at all.

38

The day Lehi slipped from the front page of the *Deseret News* the weather changed drastically, like it sometimes does in April, winter into summer without transition. A shirt-sleeve crowd walked the sidewalks in front of the temple. Every few minutes a tour bus pulled up, adding to the throng. Invariably, all new arrivals craned their heads toward Moroni's tower before moving through the gates and onto the temple grounds.

In the midst of it all, Mad Bill strolled along in one of his light summer robes, parting rubberneckers as he went. He wore a new sandwich board: MORONI LIVES.

Traveler waved from his open window. But Bill, intent on his mission, didn't look up.

Traveler took a deep breath. The smell of sycamore leaves, their fragrance set free by the recent crush of snow, promised rebirth.

His father was seated at the desk, making out a bill to send to Penny Varney.

When Traveler saw the total he said, "We'll take it out of the advance Willis gave me."

"Oh, no. That's church money. It goes back."

"You can give it back to Willis yourself. He's due here any minute."

"I'm leaving, then," Martin answered, pushing back from the desk and stepping to the door. But when he opened it Penny was already standing there, with Willis Tanner right behind her.

Penny rushed inside to hug Traveler. "We're on our way to the temple," she said excitedly. "But we had to stop by and thank you first." She glanced over her shoulder at Tanner. Her possessive smile was that of an admiring disciple.

"Actually," Willis said, "the prophet sent us. He wants to apologize for not being able to thank you in person."

"Your people kept my name out of it. That's thanks enough."

"There is something you can do," Martin said.

"Name it," Tanner said.

"What did you find in Moroni's trumpet?"

Smiling broadly, Tanner looked from father to son. "You didn't really expect us to find anything, did you?"

Penny broke the silence that followed. "I have something for you, Mr. Traveler." She dug into her purse and brought out an envelope.

Traveler shook his head. "If that's money, you're going to need it for lawyers."

"Oh, no. There isn't going to be any trial. Isn't that right, Will?"

Tanner took hold of her hand and squeezed it reassuringly. "From now on John Varney is in the hands of psychiatrists."

"God help him, then," Martin said, taking charge

of the envelope. To Tanner he added, "You have a refund coming."

Tanner shook his head. "There's more to come. A bonus. It was the least the prophet could do to show his gratitude."

"We won't spend it," Martin said.

"That's up to you. Now, if you'll excuse us, we're due at the temple."

Penny grabbed Traveler and embraced him again. "Will has arranged everything. We're baptizing my mother."

Traveler was still trying to think of something to say when they left. Behind him the phone rang. His father answered, "Moroni Traveler and Son."

Traveler shook his head. He didn't feel like talking.

"Yes, he's here," Martin said, handing him the phone.

Traveler grimaced.

"It's me," Claire said. "I'm still lost."

About the Author

Robert Irvine is the author of two horror novels and seven mysteries, two of which were nominated for the Edgar Allan Poe Award by the Mystery Writers of America. Like the hero of *BAPTISM FOR THE DEAD*, Robert Irvine was born in Salt Lake City, Utah. He now resides with his wife in Carmel, California, where he is at work on his next Moroni Traveler mystery.

Look for *THE ANGEL'S SHARE*, Robert Irvine's next mystery coming from POCKET BOOKS.